Inadvertent

Valor

by

Arley L. Dial

A western novel

Copyright © 2012 Arley L. Dial

All rights reserved.

ISBN: **1503079376**
ISBN-13: **978-1503079373**

Table of Contents

Chapter 1

Know dear reader, that between the time when the rebels bombed Fort Sumpter and the rise of the Wright brothers there was a time undreamed of. Vast prairies were populated by primitive tribes, cyclopean mountains were inhabited by naught but wild beasts, and mighty rivers ran unchecked thorough the land. But the proudest territory in the west was Arizona, reining supreme in the dreaming west. Hither came Alouicious Rucker the Tennessean, black haired, sullen eyed, pistol in hand, with gigantic melancholies and gigantic mirth, to tread the silver fields beneath his booted heel.

--excerpt from "Al Rucker: a Western Legend" by Peabody Samuelson

"I hear there's silver in the Arizona territory, there for the taking" Almer said as he stepped through the door onto the rickety porch of the cabin swirling the coffee dregs in the bottom of his tin cup before drinking it down, "Though I haven't seen it myself."

The old man smoothed what was left of his short gray hair before covering it with a hat which was perfectly shaped to his skull through many seasons of wear. His homespun shirt and pants, which might have been of discernable color once, had faded to become the grayish tan that all clothes did after so much wearing with too few washings.

"Just lying around like they say gold used to be in California?" Alouicious Rucker asked casually, as if he hadn't heard the stories for himself. The thin, young man wore a pair of overalls which had apparently loyally served generations of his family and a shapeless hat which, judging by the salt encrusting the band, had seen too many days working on a humid Tennessee farm. Alouicious had an open honest face, with expressive blue eyes which gave him a guileless look that tempted some unscrupulous people to take advantage of him.

"They say you have to do some digging to get to it, but there's plenty of it Ruck," Almer replied using the nickname Alouicious had gone by since he was a boy. Almer had known the Rucker family since he had settled in the area years before, and had seen Ruck grow from a gangly brown haired boy into the slightly less gangly brown haired man before him. When Ruck's father left to fight the Yankees, Almer had been neighborly, helping Ruck look after his two younger sisters and work the small plot of land and few head of stock that made up the family farm. It saddened Almer a little that Ruck had had to grow up so quickly, but an orphan in a war torn land had little choice and so Almer had done his best to advise Ruck as the boy dealt with matters which only a grown man should have to consider.

Almer had been quite a traveler in his younger days, trapping beaver in the Rockies and occasionally scouting for the army before old age had driven him back east of the Mississippi to settle in Tennessee. He had spent many long hours regaling the young Alouicious with stories of his adventures in the wilderness, and thus he felt somewhat responsible for Ruck's recent decision to abandon his boyhood home and head west seeking an adventure of his own.

Ruck's sisters had both married veterans shortly after the war, leaving him alone, and with strife and privation still prevailing on the land despite the fact that Tennessee had been readmitted to the Union years earlier, the Rucker family farm was paying fewer and fewer dividends every year. Ruck did not have enough money to hire any help and though a hard worker he found himself unequal to the task of making the farm pay as each year the crop he was able to bring in had brought less profit than the year before.

When Ruck had first heard the reports of silver in the southwest, he had disregarded the claims as so much folderol, but as the farm lost more and more money, the prospect of trying his luck in the silver fields had become more attractive. The tales Almer had told him over the years had sown the seeds of wanderlust in him, and news that huge sums of money were being made in the silver fields had cultivated the idea until Ruck had decided to pull up stakes and head west to try his luck in a land where men were drawing vast fortunes from the sandy hills of the Indian infested Arizona Territory.

"The folks I sold the place to will be around today or tomorrow," said Ruck, changing the subject to more practical and immediate matters. "Rosalie and Bess are gonna be mad as wet hens when they find out who I sold the place to" He said, a wry grin emerging through the sparse beginnings of a dark beard.

Ruck had sold the house and most of the stock to a Negro family who had come around a few weeks before asking if there was any land for sale in the area. He didn't know if they had been slaves before the war and had not asked, but when he heard the family was in the market for a small farm, he had quickly offered his own. Ruck knew that his sisters would be scandalized at the very thought of a Negro family moving into their childhood home, and he was enchanted by the idea of confounding his sisters one last time before he headed west and could be shut of them for good.

"I guess they'll either get over it or they won't," the old man said matching his companion's grin tooth for tooth.

"Even so, I'd rather be far away when they find out, them girls are mean as snakes" said Ruck, with a shudder. Rosalie and Bess were of a sour disposition even during the best of times, mercilessly tormenting Ruck as a matter of course. Ruck had been around a few children and knew of their capacity for cruelty inflicted in the name of fun, but Rosalie and Bess seemed to see malice as their duty and spite as their calling in life. Nor was Ruck the only recipient of their constant vitriol; neighbors, fellow churchgoers, farmyard animals, sometimes even the very wind and water seemed to suffer abuse at his siblings' hands. Often Ruck had wondered how they had both managed to find husbands. The men who married his sisters must have been terribly traumatized by the horrors of Gettysburg and Bull Run to find life with his sisters tolerable. His father had died fighting against the Union, and Ruck figured that it wouldn't be long before his sisters' husbands wished that they had met a similar fate.

"Indeed they are. It's a shame they don't take after your dear departed mother," Almer said, his tone becoming wistful. "She was a kind soul."

"She sure was," whispered Ruck, his tone echoing the old man's. "Damn but I can't abide cows!"

Almer chuckled at Ruck's seemingly incongruous outburst, but his mirth went unnoticed as the young man's misty gaze was still far away. Just before the war claimed his father, Ruck's mother had been killed in a freak milking accident. Being just a boy, Ruck developed an unreasoning fear of the federal government, and the entire bovine species, both of which he considered mindless ravening monsters. Ruck had loved his mother and father very much, and when he was a boy it seemed there was no obstacle that couldn't be overcome by their kind ways and relentless work ethic, but that sense of security had been stripped away by an overfed, heartless beast and a milk cow. A grown man with the twin fears of cattle and government would be humorous if they hadn't been born of such senseless tragedies. Well, maybe it was a little funny anyhow, Almer thought.

"You reckon to make it all the way to Arizona on Bolliver?" inquired Almer, Shifting his attention to Ruck's mule which was cropping the weeds around the porch. The mule in question raised his head and looked at the two men as if responding to his name being spoken. The gray mule appeared slightly comical, with some of the weeds he had been sampling still sticking out of his mouth, but the two men knew better than to be fooled by appearances.

Bolliver continually displayed an eerie intelligence which was unsettling to some people, especially those he had outwitted, of which there were more than a few. Ruck had purchased Bolliver a few years before for a surprisingly small sum. At first he was suspicious of the low price, but after a thorough inspection, Ruck could find nothing wrong with the animal and happily accepted the bargain. Over the next few weeks Ruck began to suspect that Bolliver's previous owners had been disquieted by the mule's incredible intelligence and constant calculation which Ruck had to admit was disturbing at times. Ruck would never have imagined that a beast could look at someone with contempt, but when he saw the mule looking at Rosalie and Bess, that was the only way he could describe it. That was why Ruck took such a shine to the mule. In Bolliver he had finally found an ally. He smiled at the memory of Rosalie shouting imprecations at Bolliver while Bess whacked him on the rump with a stick, and the mule *sneering* before lifting his tail to do his equine business in the garden path.

"I reckon he'll make it all right, I'm not taking much, just a bedroll and a few odds and ends." Ruck said, indicating the bundle tied behind Bolliver's saddle. "Besides, I plan on taking a steamer up to St. Louis and then a train west from there so we won't be walking across half the country." Ruck's small life savings and the pittance he had received from the sale of his childhood home were tucked away in his saddle bags beside the few possibles he had deemed necessary for the trip. He planned to travel light, saving his money as best he could, until he could find a likely place to try his hand at prospecting somewhere in the west. Tales of the Arizona territory had intrigued him and it seemed as good a place as any to head for, as recent reports of rich lodes of silver and gold had been coming from the area for some time.

"They say the west is still a fairly wild place. The

Cavalry hasn't got hold of the Apache yet, and prospectors and gamblers are scattered from hell to breakfast."

Ruck had heard the same thing. When the war of Northern aggression broke out, most of the soldiers had left Arizona to fight back east, giving the Apache a free hand in a region known as "Apacheria" which encompassed much of New Mexico and Arizona. Silver was discovered in paying quantities and almost immediately droves of prospectors flooded into the dangerous region and were followed in turn by gamblers, outlaws and conmen of every sort, last in the stampede would be law and civilization, and Ruck hoped to reach Arizona long before that happened.

"You might need a pistol in country like that." said Almer, reaching through the doorway to retrieve something hanging beside the door. "That rifle your pa gave you is a good one but this will be better for close up work." Almer handed Ruck a holstered pistol wrapped in a belt. Ruck was speechless. Drawing the pistol from the holster, he saw that it was an older revolver which had clearly seen long use but had been lovingly cared for by its previous owner. The rough leather holster was shiny in spots from rubbing against a pant leg or sleeve and the pistol itself, though slightly tarnished, was free of the patina of rust which was common in the humid climate of Tennessee. Checking the load, he noticed that the pistol had been converted from its original cap and ball design to accept the same ammunition as his lever action rifle.

"I can't take this, Almer. It's too much" stammered Ruck, uncomfortable with such a lavish gift.

"Nonsense boy, I don't need the thing, I've had it a year and ain't shot it once. One of the confederate boys was passing through on his way home, down on his luck, so I traded him some dry goods and possibles for it. It was charity at the time, and charity it will stay, I got no use for a fancy iron like that, but where you're going you're liable to need it."

Still touched by his old friend's generosity, Ruck buckled the belt around his waist and tried to find a comfortable resting place for the unfamiliar weight.

"Well thanks, old man. Thanks for everything." Ruck said as he shook Almer's hand and stepped off the porch.

"Good luck Alouicious." said Almer, raising his hand in farewell, "It surely has been a blessing knowing you."

Ruck unhitched and mounted Bolliver, touching the brim of his hat as he turned toward the road, not trusting his voice to remain steady enough to reply as he rode away from one of his dearest friends for the last time.

"Bolliver, you take care of the boy, you hear?"

Almer hollered after them. The mule did not deign to reply.

Two days later, a wet and miserable Ruck sat hunched against the wind and rain on the leeward side of a hill, while Bolliver stood a little way off cropping grass and looking forlorn. During the war, the barns had been torn or burnt down and all the trees cut to make railroad ties or corduroy roads resulting in a decided lack of natural shelter and leaving Ruck at the mercy of the elements, which currently consisted of steady drizzling rain and a swirling, inescapable wind. Ruck chewed his supper of jerky and hard tack, both hard and flavorless, with the resignation of someone who had never been picky about what he ate and imagined the dry warmth of the western deserts.

Another shift in the wind brought a strong smell wafting toward him and Ruck looked over his shoulder to see a shaggy pie-bald dog with its head raised trying to catch the scent of the camp. Ruck turned back to his meager meal thinking the dog would head back to wherever it came from, but soon the dog had circled around in front of him questing back and forth, clearly curious but hesitant to approach the camp. The dog was of indefinable breed, mostly white with black and brown patches here and there, but its head was all black, looking as if a black dog's head had somehow been attached to a pie-bald dog's body. It occurred to Ruck that the mangy beast was possibly the ugliest mongrel he had ever laid eyes on. Ruck had difficulty making out whether the dog was well fed or poor due to its shaggy, heavily matted coat, but he assumed it was as hungry as most things were in this part of the country. Ruck didn't react to the dog's presence as it cautiously made its way closer, and when the dog got close enough, Ruck was struck by the soulful brown eyes staring at him from a pathetically wet face.

"Here ye go Whitey." Ruck said as he pitched the dog a good sized piece of hard tack. Whitey sniffed the offering before snatching it up and gobbling it down as curs are wont to do. The cold wet dog wagged its shaggy tail a few times slinging foul smelling water over the camp and moved closer to the cold wet man, neither one suspecting the repercussions that small act of kindness would have on their lives.

Chapter 2

Astride his mighty charger whose thews and hooves described the very meaning of haste, and accompanied by his sleek, obedient hound which scouted to the fore alert, wary of any threat to his master, Rucker emerged from the mist of the Appalachian Mountains bringing nobility and justice to the untamed west.

--excerpt from "Al Rucker: a Western Legend" by Peabody Samuelson.

Whitey ran under Bolliver's belly for perhaps the tenth time that day, causing the mule to shy sideways attempting to kick the dog, jostling Ruck in the saddle.

"Confound it you two! Can't a man ride in peace for an hour without you horsing around?" groused Ruck, sawing the reins to bring Bolliver back under control.

Having recovered from his brief bout of shyness, Whitey had become friendly and playful, taking great sport in tormenting Bolliver by sprinting beneath the mule while barking sharply before emerging from the other side to turn at bay and pose with his head on his forepaws, his tail wagging triumphantly in the air. The dog appeared to take great joy in the game, but the mule was obviously not amused, sending retaliatory kicks toward the dog any time the opportunity presented itself. Whitey seemed to anticipate every attack though, ducking and dodging Bolliver's murderous hooves before circling wide and pausing only briefly before charging back in for another pass.

Ruck had enjoyed the journey through Tennessee despite the antics of his companions as the rolling green hills and soothing morning mist heralded adventure and salved the young man's wanderlust. With few exceptions the weather had treated them well, with only the occasional cold spring shower to dampen man and beast, and no great trouble had assailed them as they made their way west.

The land and communities they passed were slow to recover from the destruction of war however, and Ruck was struck by the deprivation which was often clearly visible around them. Shabbily dressed sod busters goaded jaded mules and oxen to drag rusty plows through the earth in preparation for the spring planting, as barefoot children went about the familiar tasks of daily survival on a struggling farm. The homesteads he passed seemed to be dilapidated and Ruck felt empathy toward the hard working people as he knew the despair of working through the long year only to find that there was barely enough money left over to purchase necessities, much less improve or repair anything. Ruck respected the stubborn determination he saw on the faces of those he passed, while at the same time feeling relieved to have left the life of bare subsistence behind him.

Anxious to be in a place that hadn't suffered so much devastation, he lengthened his days in the saddle, breaking camp before daylight and riding long after the sun had set setting as quick a pace as he felt Bolliver could tolerate. Ruck soon drew near to Memphis and the mighty Mississippi River, where he hoped to find a riverboat that would carry him upriver to St. Louis. Ruck had heard that river traffic was not what it was before the war, as railroads had come to dominate the movement of freight in the region, but he still hoped to find a river captain willing to make room for Bolliver and himself (and apparently Whitey) since he had long wished to experience a trip along the Mississippi River he had heard so much about.

As he wended his way through the countryside outside Memphis, Ruck recalled some of Almer's stories of the wide open spaces, majestic countryside and wild characters of the west, dreamily anticipating seeing them with his own eyes. So deep was his reverie that he was caught off guard when Whitey chose that moment to leap off a steep roadside embankment to land nimbly behind Bolliver's saddle. The proud mule decided he would have no part in such indignity and promptly sat down, spilling Ruck and Whitey into the dusty road.

Ruck was not a man given to cursing, but he was sorely tempted to become one as he picked himself up out of the dirt and brushed himself off.

"My first stop in Memphis is liable to be the soap factory if you two don't cut it out," Ruck grumbled, eyeing Bolliver and Whitey dangerously. "I don't know if they'll render a cur but we'll soon find out" Ruck moved to gather the reins and gave them a tug to get Bolliver to stand up but the indignant mule would not budge.

"Come on you durned mule!" admonished Ruck, giving the reins a firm pull. Bolliver's head stretched forward, and his ears lay back, but his hindquarters remained defiantly planted. Whitey looked on with what could only be amusement at the antics of man and mule until his ears perked up and he shifted his attention up the road. The steep embankment and a curve in the road meant that one couldn't see far, but Whitey continued his vigil, cocking his head to the side and giving a short bark. Ruck's struggles and imprecations to get Bolliver to his feet increased, causing the mule to bray, and the combined noise masked the sound of hooves thundering up the road to all but canine ears.

Around the bend sprinted a dun horse, its rider leaning forward yet looking behind him. Seeing the tableau of Ruck and Bolliver struggling in the road at the last second, the dun horse planted his front feet and turned on a dime, leaping to gain the top of the embankment from which Whitey had jumped just a few minutes before. The horse's rider, looking back as he was, was woefully unprepared for such an abrupt maneuver and instantly lost the saddle, landing heavily in the dust at Ruck's feet.

"Now look what you did you jug-headed mule!" cried Ruck as he crouched to see to the stunned man. "You might have killed him!"

The man on the ground groaned as Ruck dashed to the saddle to get his canteen. Not knowing what else to do, he poured some water into his hand and daubed it onto the stricken man's forehead. The stunned man had heavy features, with a prodigious brow and strong stubble encrusted chin, he wore store-bought clothes on his large well-formed frame which seemed fancy to Ruck's eyes and boots which still bore much of the original shine, lacking the scuffed appearance of a working man's footwear. The man's eyes fluttered and he groaned again, his senses slow to return after such a jarring impact on the ground.

"You took a bad spill there mister; best just lay still for a minute," at the sound of Ruck's voice, the man's eyes snapped open and he began to struggle to gain his feet. "Now just settle down there, it sounds like you lost your wind, best just lie back" implored Ruck, but the man seemed addled, and continued to try to gain his feet, even as he wheezed for air.

Over the sounds of the man's distress Ruck began to hear the distinctive rumble of hooves thundering up the road. Fearing another wreck, Ruck grasped the man's wrists and dragged him toward the roadside. Bolliver, also hearing the horses, ambled his way off to the other side, which was less steep and played host to some rather toothsome looking greenery.

Around the bend came a group of half a dozen riders at a gentle lope. They drew up short and much to Ruck's dismay each of them leveled a weapon at the two men on the ground.

"Step away from that man, kid, and keep your hands up" the foremost rider ordered. Ruck slowly raised his hands and stepped back, noticing with some guilty relief that most of the riders' guns remained trained on the man on the ground. "Will, get on down there and collect those pistols." A small man with a prodigious goatee dismounted, and strode toward Ruck and the man. The fallen man was disarmed first. He seemed to be regaining both his breath and his senses, yet he made no move to rise as Ruck quietly relinquished his pistol to the man holding the shotgun.

"Now what the hell's going on here?" asked the lead rider, pointing his rifle at Ruck. Having never had a gun pointed at him before, the muzzle of the rifle looked huge, its black maw eclipsing the world and causing everything else to seem less real by comparison.

"I had trouble with my mule, sir" stammered Ruck. "We was standing in the road when this fellow came around the corner riding hell bent for leather and took a spill. It was an accident, I swear" said Ruck, his eyes never leaving the cavernous barrel pointed at him.

The rider chuckled as he raised the muzzle of his rifle. The world seemed to swim back into focus for Ruck, who got a good look at the man with the rifle for the first time. He was a well dressed heavyset man, with a flushed complexion and sweat running down his jowls from heat or excitement, possibly both. The man sported a thin, rather sad looking white mustache and had a star pinned to his vest. Ruck was amazed at how something as obvious as a shiny tin star can be obscured by something as small as the muzzle of a rifle.

"Do you have any idea who this man is, son?" asked the marshal, indicating the man who still lay on the ground.

"Nossir" replied Ruck, puzzled at the turn of the conversation.

"Why that's Logan Beckwith, the outlaw bank robber. We've been trying to catch him since the end of the war!"

After securing the outlaw Beckwith to his horse, which hadn't run far, and returning Ruck's pistol, the posse headed back toward Memphis. Ruck mounted Bolliver (who in the excitement had given up his protest against traveling with such an obnoxious dog) and rode alongside the marshal, who introduced himself as Bob Calloway.

"It sure was lucky for us that you had that trouble with your mule when you did," said Marshal Calloway, "we would have lost Beckwith for sure if you hadn't. That fellow back there has gotten very good at getting away from a posse over the years." After the war, some of the guerilla fighters had turned to a life of crime, committing robberies against what the unreconstructed rebels saw as "Union" banks, and were lauded by some rural folks for not submitting to Northern oppression. Not the Beckwith gang however, for their depredations ran the gamut of Northern and Southern enterprises, rich or poor, no one was safe from the Beckwith Gang, whose name had become a byword in Tennessee, Arkansas and Missouri.

Logan Beckwith himself, leader of the gang, had evaded capture when anyone else would have long ago been caught, seeming to melt into the landscape at will. Today the dreaded outlaw seemed to have slipped up though, robbing a saloon in broad daylight, just blocks from the marshal's office and leading a readymade posse of deputies on a merry chase thorough town, before heading up the road where he had the misfortune to run afoul of a mule that was pissed off at a dog.

"What kind of trouble did you say you had? That mule looks fine now." asked the marshal glancing at Bolliver.

"Not trouble so much," replied Ruck reddening slightly as his gaze shifted to Whitey, who was fertilizing the brush by the side of the road. "Just checking my load, I didn't know how far it was into town."

"Memphis is just a mile or two from where you were, we're about there now," said Marshal Calloway wondering what the young man was not telling him.

Riding into the city, the posse was greeted by hails from passers by as it was seen that the dreaded Logan Beckwith was finally captured. Marshal Calloway invited Ruck to come to the calaboose and take a cup of coffee saying that it was the least he could do for the man who had helped capture a notorious outlaw, so Ruck rode along with them grateful for the chance to relax with a hot cup of coffee after the morning's excitement.

The genial atmosphere of the posse's triumphant entry into Memphis was shattered though as sudden shots rang out from a bank on the corner. The startled, but still heavily armed posse turned eyes and guns toward the bank just as four men wearing neckerchiefs over their faces and brandishing pistols spilled from the bank and moved toward their horses. Seeing the posse gathered in the street in front of them the robbers paused, and for a moment it was a frozen tableau as the startled bank robbers found themselves under the gaze of an equally startled group of lawmen.

Whitey, who could sense the tension but could not discern its source, let out a sharp bark as if giving the signal for all hell to break loose. God himself would be hard pressed to determine who shot first as smoke and fire billowed forth from the muzzles of several guns at once. The first volley went in all directions as both sides found themselves in a furious gunfight at a moment's notice. Bolliver took off like a shot, silently praying to whomever mules pray to that the damned dog would get shot. Ruck was thrown from the saddle and knocked senseless as the mule went from a standing start to lightning speed in the blink of an eye. The chaos of panicking horses and flying lead continued, and before long, two of the bandits were down, creased by the deputies' bullets and the other two decided that discretion was the better part of valor and dropped their irons in surrender.

When the smoke cleared, no one had been killed, but two of the outlaws and one of the deputies would need the not so tender ministrations of the local saw bones. Ruck, who had spent most of the fight lying on his back was roused by a horrible carrion stench which turned out to be Whitey's breath as he licked Ruck's face.

"I figure Beckwith robbed that saloon to get us to chase him and draw us away from his boys who were fixing to hit the bank." said Marshal Calloway after they had locked up the gang. "It was double lucky for us he ran into you on the trail. They would have had us coming and going."

"Just an accident really," replied Ruck, wincing at the horrible taste which has been the hallmark of police station coffee since time immemorial.

"Just the same though, without you we never would have caught them, you deserve some reward. Here's a hundred dollars. It's not all that was offered, but like you say it was an accident."

"Much obliged, marshal." Ruck said, graciously accepting the coins while declining a refill of the awful coffee. "Do you reckon it's too late to catch a riverboat today? I'm anxious to get upriver."

"Oh you'll have no trouble finding somebody going north, river traffic is fairly heavy this time of year." replied the marshal. "Come back and visit if the Arizona Territory doesn't agree with you, I'd hate for you to think that Memphis is nothing but shooting scrapes and outlaws."

With that, Ruck took his leave of the Marshal, lighthearted, knowing that the first leg of his journey was over. Pockets flush with extra cash, his outlook was so optimistic he didn't notice the baleful glare that

Logan Beckwith cast his way from behind the bars of the jail cell.

Chapter 3

Mysterious stranger captures Outlaw Gang!

The Notorious Beckwith Gang was captured yesterday in Memphis, after a cunning attempt to rob both the saloon and the bank at the same time was foiled by a mysterious stranger. Marshal Calloway told this reporter that Logan Beckwith, the leader of the dreaded gang, was brought low outside town by a man calling himself Alouicious Rucker, who then led the posse back to Memphis just in time to subdue the rest of the gang. Marshal Calloway, whose attempts to curtail the activities of dastardly Beckwith gang have been thwarted for years, was quoted as saying "We wouldn't have got them if it were not for Alouicious Rucker."

--excerpt from The Memphis Daily Appeal
March 13, 1875

Logan Beckwith sat in the calaboose, outwardly calm yet seething with internal rage as a newspaper reporter interviewed Marshal Calloway. The deputies had put Logan in a cell by himself, separating him from the two uninjured members of his gang. The deputies were justified in their caution, for long had Logan Beckwith evaded justice, doing what he pleased, going where he wanted, and the law had never even been close to catching him, and now that they had him they weren't about to let go.

During the War Between the States, Logan and his gang had never declared for one side or the other, roving through the Border States, robbing and killing who they would and letting guerillas from one side or the other take the blame. Things had been a little trickier since the cessation of hostilities, but with the country still in shambles, there was plenty of opportunity for a man like Beckwith to prosper. And Logan desperately needed to prosper.

The reason for that need was a St. Louis actress named Flora Calhoun. Nearly a year before, Logan had been in Nashville taking in a traveling show when Flora walked on stage and his life had changed forever. Most people would have described Flora as a short, rather plump woman with thick brown hair and plain features, but the moment he laid eyes on her Logan knew she was the only woman for him. The Nashville newspaper had later described her performance as rather pedestrian, but Logan had been entranced while she was on stage, and upon her exit he had given her a one man standing ovation. After the show he had finagled his way backstage to be introduced to the actress who had ensnared his heart.

The outlaw who had robbed fortified banks up and down the Mississippi was shocked to find that the dressing room of a two bit actress was nigh impenetrable, as a huge man with no discernable neck and hands like scoop shovels guarded her door politely refusing him entry, but offering to relay a message to Miss Calhoun.

"Tell her that I enjoyed her show a great deal, and would be honored to meet her," said Logan, irritated at having to grovel before a flunky, but desperate to introduce himself.

The large man knocked on the door lightly and disappeared into the dressing room for mere moments before emerging once more into the hallway.

"I'm sorry sir, but Miss Calhoun is not receiving visitors at this time" said the guard in surprisingly genteel tones for one who could have made a living wrestling bears.

"When the hell will she be receiving visitors?" asked Logan growing agitated.

"Perhaps when the visitor brings a suitable gift," whispered the massive thug conspiratorially.

"Where am I supposed to get a gift for a woman at this time of night?" grumbled Logan.

"I see your difficulty, sir" said the big man not unkindly "the troupe will be returning to St. Louis in the morning for a four month engagement and I recommend you take in the show if you happen to be in town. Incidentally, Miss Calhoun has a fondness for fancy gloves and handkerchiefs."

Opening night of the play in St. Louis the next week found Logan in the front row with a box containing the finest kid gloves money could buy and an array of scented lace handkerchiefs resting on the seat next to him. The big man, whose name turned out to be Buford, had taken the box into the dressing room and emerged with an invitation to meet Miss Calhoun.

Thus began the courtship of Miss Flora Calhoun by the outlaw Logan Beckwith. Over the following months, Logan had spent every penny he had and every penny he could steal on progressively more expensive gifts for the love of his life. His every thought was bent to the purpose of winning her hand, and he had thought the prize was in his grasp until the day he found out he had a rival.

Logan had arrived at the door to Flora's dressing room struggling with a large unwieldy box only to be stopped by Buford.

"Sorry Logan, but Miss Calhoun is entertaining Senator Bradley at the moment, you'll have to come back later" said Buford.

"Senator Bradley? What is he doing in there?" asked an enraged Logan.

"I'm sure I don't know, but he brought pearl earrings with him" replied Buford.

"Pearl earrings?"

"Yup,"

"Dang,"

Logan's first instinct had been to draw his pistol and kick down the door, but even he couldn't expect to get away with gunning down a sitting senator and riding away with Flora thrown over the cantle of his saddle like some barbarian raider, so he had relented and turned away, rejection weighing heavily on his shoulders.

The next night he had returned with several more boxes piled upon the first, and this time Flora had been alone.

"Oh, the senator has been very kind," said Flora casually, after Buford had ushered him into the cluttered dressing room. "And I should tell you that he has asked for my hand in marriage. A man like him has ever so many prospects."

"Prospects? I've got more prospects than I know what to do with!" shouted Logan.

"What kind of prospects does an outlaw have to match those of a senator?" asked Flora cutting Logan to the quick.

"Give me one week, and I'll have enough to set us up for life. Just give me a chance, Flora" Logan pleaded.

"Very well Logan, you have one week to show me that you can provide for me, then we shall see," said Flora with rather less commitment than Logan would have preferred.

"You'll see my dear, we'll be as rich as creosote," said Logan, and as he rose to leave, his mind was already racing with plans of a daring daylight robbery which would secure the heart and hand of the woman he loved.

Now instead of riding triumphantly into St. Louis to claim his prize, he was stuck in the Memphis jailhouse all because of some hayseed and his cursed mule.

The thunderheads of rage and frustration within Beckwith's mind turned black at the thought of the hillbilly who had been the author of his downfall. With his gang locked up or injured and his plans in ruins he had no time to secure the money he needed to appease Flora before she accepted the senator's proposal, and then and there he silently swore that if Alouicious Rucker had ruined his chance to marry the woman he loved he would get revenge or die in the attempt. The first order of business was escape, but little could be done in plain view of the marshal and the reporter, so he turned his attention to their conversation in an attempt to glean what information he could about his foe.

"So you didn't actually see what happened between Beckwith and this young man Rucker?" asked Peabody Samuelson reporter for the Memphis Daily Appeal, with his pencil and pad at the ready.

"No, when we came around the bend, Beckwith was already lying in the road at Rucker's feet." replied Marshal Calloway.

"Amazing!" breathed Peabody, "What type of weapon did the man have?"

"He carried a pistol to the best of my recollection, but it was holstered when I first saw him." the marshal said.

"So this Rucker unhorsed and subdued the most notorious outlaw in the state without so much as drawing his gun?" inquired the reporter, scribbling furiously on his tablet.

"Now I'm not sure that's how it happened." said Calloway with a frown.

"But you said yourself, that you found Beckwith

lying senseless on the ground at Rucker's feet. He had to have beaten one of the most dangerous men in the state with his bare hands." Said Peabody as his pencil filled line after line out of all proportion to what few facts the marshal was actually supplying.

Peabody Samuelson was a rather slight, bookish man, with the pale, soft look of one who spent their days reading and writing in dim indoor light. The reporter had the kind of face which made one think he was wearing spectacles even though he did not, and had curly brown hair which showed gray at the temples. He wore a neat brown suit with matching bowler hat which spoke of a fastidious man, not rich but with pride in what little he did have.

Peabody had become a reporter for the Memphis Daily Appeal during the war, and had spent most of the time barely missing being the one to describe the many tales of heroism the conflict had generated. Every battle, every action, every shift in the political wind, Peabody had arrived just in time to be the last one to hear about it. But now he finally had the scoop. A mysterious stranger riding into town (no doubt on a magnificent steed) and single handedly capturing a man who had stymied the authorities for years was a story he longed to be the first to write. So great was that longing, that a little thing like facts could hardly be expected to contend with it.

"What about the rest of the Beckwith gang? I

see you have two of them here, but I understand there were four who tried to rob the bank." Peabody asked the Marshal.

"Two of them were wounded along with Deputy Browder in the fight outside the bank, they're over at Dr. Ellsworth's place now under guard." replied Calloway.

"Is it safe to say that if Alouicious Rucker hadn't captured Logan Beckwith, that you would still be chasing him and therefore unable to stop the bank robbery?" the reporter asked with the utter lack of shame only a reporter can achieve.

"I can't begin to speculate on what would have happened if Beckwith hadn't come across Rucker when he did." Marshal Calloway replied, instinctively stonewalling the newspaperman as all good police officers do.

"Where is this Rucker now?" Peabody asked the Marshal.

"He said he was headed upriver to St. Louis." said Marshal Calloway, clearly enunciating in an attempt to insert at least one solid fact into the drivel that the hack reporter was surely producing. "From there he was going to take a train west I believe."

"Thank you Marshal, you've been most helpful." said Peabody, abruptly grabbing up his satchel and making for the door. "I have to get a statement from him before he leaves town. What kind of horse does he ride?"

"Oh, there's no mistaking that gray of his." replied Marshal Calloway, valiantly keeping a straight face until the door closed, and Peabody was gone.

While Calloway and Peabody spoke, Beckwith's rage only grew. Not a man given to explosive fury, Logan's anger simmered beneath the surface, congealing and focusing on the man named Alouicious Rucker. The totality of Beckwith's mind was bent to the purpose of avenging himself on the man who had robbed him of his only chance to win Flora, but the outlaw who had planned and carried out so many outrageous heists was not a man of rash action.

"First things first," whispered Beckwith, as he turned his attention to the grate of bars over the window of his cell and considered his means of escape, waiting for the perfect moment with rattlesnake patience.

Peabody Samuelson returned to the office of the Memphis Daily Appeal tired and dejected. His inquiries at the docks about a powerfully built man riding a mighty grey horse had borne no fruit and the only stranger he had seen had been a lad clearly just down from the hills leading a mule which was being harassed by a ragged looking dog. He had finally given up the search and headed back to the office to finish the article for the next day's paper. It was almost sundown, and the office was empty as Peabody slumped into his chair and began to arrange his notes about the capture of the Beckwith Gang. Peabody couldn't shake the feeling that this story, with such a heroic character at its core would be his opus, but without an interview with Rucker, the story would ring hollow. Sighing in resignation, Peabody began to type the body of the article on the machine the newspaper had recently purchased from a Wisconsin company. For many hours, the clicking of the typewriter keys was the only sound in the lonely office.

Peabody was startled awake when his editor Mr. Johnson crashed through the door of the office.

"Peabody! I just heard the Marshal has the Beckwith gang in the calaboose!" shouted Johnson "What are you doing here? Get over there and get a statement from Calloway!"

Still groggy from falling asleep at his desk, Peabody wiped the drool from the corner of his mouth and looked up at his boss through bleary eyes. Mr. Ronald F. Johnson, editor of the Memphis Daily appeal, was an excitable older man with a totally bald head and gaunt features which made him look like a vulture wearing spectacles. For a man of such advanced age, he seemed to have an endless supply of energy which he used primarily to browbeat his employees. Peabody had suffered through Mr. Johnson's tirades for many years though, and was unfazed by the editor's onslaught.

"Already done sir, I have the story here," mumbled Peabody withdrawing the page from the typewriter.

Robbed of some of his bluster, Mr. Johnson perused the page as Peabody rubbed his eyes and shook the cobwebs from his head.

"This is good Peabody, but we need a statement from this Rucker fellow, where is he now?" asked Mr. Johnson.

"Marshal Calloway said he was headed north on a riverboat, so I went to the docks to find him but no one had seen him," replied Peabody, "So I came back here to finish what I had before the typesetters got here."

"This is good work, but we still need a statement from Rucker, and we need it quick" mused Johnson, "After they hang Beckwith people won't care anymore, so pack a bag Peabody, you've got to get to St. Louis and find this man. Keep your receipts, but I'm not paying for any whiskey or sporting women!"

His hope for the story of a lifetime rekindled, Peabody Samuelson dashed for the door, hot on the trail of a legend.

While the reporter hurriedly packed a valise, across town in the jailhouse, Logan Beckwith made his move. During the wee hours, only one deputy was left to guard the prisoners, but he was alert despite the fact that none of his charges had spoken or so much as moved in hours. The two members of the gang were sleeping, but Beckwith himself sat on the edge of his cot with his head in his hands. With tears streaming down his face, Logan Beckwith raised his head and spoke the first words he had said since his capture.

"You wouldn't have a Bible handy would you, Deputy?" said the notorious criminal with the slightly nasal tone of a man who had been weeping.

The request shocked the deputy, who had spent many hours thinking up glib responses to requests for food, water or anything else the prisoners might ask for. The request for the Good Book took the young deputy completely off guard and he wondered at the depths of grace and mercy that could be found even in a jail cell.

Not wanting to deny a penitent man, even one so wicked as Logan Beckwith, the deputy opened the top drawer of Marshal Calloway's desk and withdrew a well thumbed and slightly foxed Bible. As the deputy approached the cell, Beckwith rose and slowly moved toward the bars, his hands trembling visibly as he approached the cell door.

Beckwith's face took on a beatific look as the

deputy slipped his hand between the bars of the cell to hand the Bible over. Quick as a snake, Logan reached past the Bible to grasp the deputy's wrist, and with a powerful yank pulled the lawman forward so hard his head struck sharply against the bars of the cell. The deputy went down as if pole axed and Logan sprang into action. Retrieving the deputy's pistol and manacles, Beckwith secured the senseless man's wrist to the bars of the cell and made sure the pistol was loaded. Methodically searching the deputy's pockets, Logan found a handkerchief and extra cartridges for the pistol, but no keys. Cursing vilely, Beckwith jammed the pistol into his belt and turned his attention back to the small window. The rage and desperation which had been building in Logan Beckwith exploded in a flurry of motion as he jumped up to grasp the exposed rafters and swung his feet forward to connect with the bars of the window. The bars, which had been fashioned in the shape of a grate and nailed to the outside of the wall gave only a little at the first blow, but Beckwith's rage wouldn't be denied. Over and over he smashed his booted feet against the grate until at last one side swung free. Logan quickly pushed the grate to the side and slipped out the window.

Having no time to waste if he was to reach Flora before she agreed to marry Senator Bradley, he ignored the members of his erstwhile gang as they cried for his help, pausing only long enough to wipe the tears and snot from his face with the deputy's handkerchief before fleeing into the night.

Yanking out nose hairs until it looked like he was crying had really hurt, and that was one more indignity he intended to make Alouicious Rucker answer for.

Chapter 4

By steamboat, train, and horseback, the mighty Alouicious Rucker traversed our great nation. Wise as a serpent and gentle as a dove, he passed amongst the righteous and the wicked alike and naught remained unchanged in his wake.

--excerpt from "Al Rucker: a Western Legend" by Peabody Samuelson.

It wasn't the gleaming white steamboat he had imagined, but after making a few inquiries, Ruck had managed to find a northbound vessel willing to make room for Bolliver and Whitey. The barge was long, sitting low in the water, and was well made despite having a rather weathered appearance. The smell of the barge was an amalgam of the varied cargoes the barge had carried over the years, the farmyard smell of fresh cut hay and not so fresh manure mixing badly with the odor of stale beer and whiskey. Filled with mostly freight, the few passengers on the barge seemed like a rough group, but Ruck didn't suspect he looked much better after his long journey across the breadth of

Tennessee, especially with a shaggy piebald dog at his heels. Bolliver had been berthed at the stern in an area set aside for stock, and seemed grateful for the solitude as Whitey remained steadfastly at Ruck's side.

Ruck gazed across the water as the sun set behind the trees lining the banks of the mighty Mississippi River and his mind created visions of the vast land to which he was bound. Throughout his childhood he had been enchanted by tales of the vast plains, towering mountains, and parched deserts. At every opportunity he would pester visitors and passing travelers for tales of the west, his minds eye filled with visions of huge herds of buffalo (which he didn't consider to be related to cows), labyrinthine canyons and pristine mountain springs. The peril of the land, which predominated the stories he heard, was part of the allure. His youthful spirit, still convinced of its own immortality, was attracted to a land filled with grizzly bears, rattlesnakes, treacherous rivers, deadly snowfalls and the barbarous tribesmen who thrived in such inhospitable climes.

To Ruck, the western bank of the Mississippi River marked the boundary of the great American West, and the soft glow of the setting sun seemed to call to him, a siren song summoning him to his rightful place in the world. He stood at the rail until the sky grew dark, luxuriating in the rare wistful moment.

Emerging from his reverie, a lighthearted Ruck

ambled toward the front of the boat where the dozen or so passengers had gathered, and saw that some were seated upon kegs surrounding a crate playing draw poker. One of the players hailed Ruck, and invited him to pull up a keg and fill out the table. Almer had taught Ruck to play poker when he was a boy, and his pockets were flush with cash from the small reward he had received from Marshal Calloway, so without hesitation, Ruck sat down, placed fifty dollars on the table and took a hand. If his mother had been alive she would never have allowed Ruck to play cards, but Ruck and Almer had whiled away many a cold winter evening with a deck of cards after supper, so Ruck felt confident that he could hold his own even among seasoned players.

Three men were hunched around the makeshift table. Two plainly dressed men, veterans of the war from the looks of their prodigious beards, were seated to either side of Ruck, but the man across the table was more sharply dressed, in a dark brown frock coat with a watch chain emerging from the breast pocket. The sharp dressed man was clean shaven, and his face was open and animated with strong features and dark hair that looked vaguely familiar to Ruck as he watched the man deal the cards. The other two seemed less jovial, and Ruck assumed that the small piles of money before them had contributed greatly to the much larger stack in front of the dealer.

Ruck played tight the first few rounds, receiving no hands worth calling an opening bet, much less openers of his own, but after a few a while he felt he had the measure of his opponents and began to loosen up. The two veterans played with a surprising lack of guile, considering most army men had played many hands during the war. The well dressed man however; who introduced himself simply as Abel, played with a guarded finesse that both impressed Ruck, and made him wary to get involved in a hand with the man.

Despite his reluctance to engage in a direct contest with the well dressed Abel, Ruck soon found that his stake was steadily depleting. He had won a few small pots off of the men to his right and left, but had taken nary a penny from the stack of coins in front of Abel, who Ruck was beginning to suspect was a professional gambler.

While the men played cards, Whitey made a circuit of the table, investigating things of interest to a cur, and angling for a scratch behind the ears or a morsel of food. Arriving beside the Abel; Whitey assumed his best soulful look and even gave a little whine which did the trick on all but the most heartless of characters. Whitey's performance was rewarded, as Abel reached into the pocket of his coat and produced a small piece of jerky which the dog accepted without hesitation.

"I would be careful feeding that dog" said Ruck, as he took his turn dealing "He can be a terrible mendicant at times."

"He's a fine looking dog" opined Abel, in blatant defiance of the evidence at hand "I bet five" he said, moving the coins into the pot.

One of the veterans called and Ruck looked down to see a pair of sevens and an ace in his hand. With only five cards in the deck that would give him significant help, the odds were poor, but Ruck's train of thought had been completely derailed by an apparently sane human being calling Whitey a 'fine looking dog' and he added his five to the pot. The other veteran quickly folded his hand, leaving three players including Ruck, to contest the hand. Abel drew two cards before reaching into his pocket to give Whitey another snack, making Ruck think he was up against a hand similar to his own, and the veteran drew three, a terrible play against Abel's clearly superior hand. Ruck took two cards, without much hope of improvement.

"I check" said Abel, rearranging the cards fanned in his hand.

"Check is good" said the veteran in turn.

Ruck looked down, and seeing that he had caught his third seven, placed a ten dollar bet, thinking his opponents had received no help. He was surprised however when the cunning Abel splashed thirty dollars into the pot. The check and raise was not always allowed in friendly games, but since no one had specified otherwise, Ruck said nothing about the unorthodox play. The veteran quickly discarded his worthless hand in the first sensible play he had made yet, and the action was to Ruck. Calling time, Ruck considered his options. He could call, hoping that Abel only had two pair, fold, fearing a higher set of trips or better, or raise, defeating the check raise bluff, which was a sophisticated play that a shrewd gambler like Abel was surely capable of. With more than fifty dollars in the pot, time seemed to slow to a crawl and the tension was palpable.

Oblivious to the drama being played out at the table, Whitey couldn't figure out why the snacks had ceased. He had tried every trick in his repertoire, the sad look and whine, the happy pant and tail wag, the loyal sit-and-gaze into the distance, all with no results. The man clearly had more jerky in his pocket, Whitey could smell it, but the men seemed to be engrossed in whatever incomprehensible activity they were engaged in, and so the frustrated Whitey decided to use a more direct method which had served him well in the past: theft. Rooting his nose into Abel's coat pocket, Whitey seized the spoils.

"Get out of there, you mangy cur!" shouted Abel abruptly, shattering the tension which prevailed over the card table. Abel yanked his coat away from Whitey and stood up, sending a clumsy kick at the dog which Whitey easily dodged.

"What's that in his mouth?" asked one of the

veterans, drawing the players and spectators attention to Whitey.

"Oh hell," whispered Abel, as his face grew pale, for sticking out of Whitey's mouth, was the prize he had seized. Far from the jerky he was hoping for, Whitey had reached into Abel's coat pocket and drawn the ace of hearts.

"Why you cheating son of a gun!" bellowed the card player to Ruck's left, while drawing a heavy pistol from his belt. Being mostly on the low end of the moral spectrum, the passengers on the riverboat rarely found themselves in a position to express righteous indignation, so they seized upon the rare opportunity with gusto. Pandemonium ensued, as spectators and card players all sprang into action at once. Abel, making a break for the freedom of the rail, was stopped cold by the grasping hands of one of the veterans and clubbed to the deck with the heavy butt of the other's pistol. Ruck was knocked off his seat by the scrum of the boat passengers who were trying to get a piece of the action and was stepped on a number of times as the press of bodies heaved to and fro. The crew of the boat waded into the melee trying to restore order while Whitey provided an accompaniment of frantic barks to the chaos. Sleeping soundly at the far end of the boat, Bolliver was jolted awake by the cacophony and quickly decided to ignore the uproar, correctly assuming that it had something to do with the wretched dog.

By the time a semblance of calm had returned to the barge, the card cheat had been stripped of all his money and heaved overboard into the river. Abel's ill gotten money was evenly distributed between the card players, and Ruck once again had made a small profit on the day. The excitement of exposing a card cheat quickly turned to exultation, and the atmosphere on the boat became festive. A bottle of low grade coffin varnish was uncorked, further adding to the merriment, as the incident was recounted over and over by those who had seen what happened to those who had not and sometimes vice versa.

Whitey, being the hero of the hour, was hailed as "the dog who could smell a cheat," and "the dog who plays poker" much to the amusement of the tipsy gathering. Throughout the night, Whitey received much adulation in the form of numerous snacks and a thorough ear scratching which he enjoyed immensely before heading to the rear of the boat to fall asleep at Bolliver's feet.

Late into the night, after the revelers had shuffled off to sleep, Ruck stood at the rail with the captain of the boat, enjoying the still night air, but the conversation about exposing the card cheat refused to die.

"I never did catch his last name" Ruck said to the Captain.

"Gave me the name of Beckwith," the Captain said. "Abel Beckwith, but I imagine he'll have to leave that one behind if he ever wants to play cards on the river again."

Abel Beckwith dragged his miserable soaking self up the eastern bank of the Mississippi and collapsed exhausted in the mud. He quickly came to the same conclusion the Captain had, knowing that his days of gambling on the river, at least for a while, were over. He stayed where he was until the sun came up and when found his bearings; he realized that he was in a familiar place. He chose his direction and struck out, hoping that his brother had stashed some dry clothes and food at his hideout which was just a few miles away.

Abel approached the clearing cautiously, knowing that if Logan was home he would likely have at least one of the boys on guard, but seeing no one he emerged from the trees and headed straight for the shack. The shack looked rather tumbledown, with a sagging roof and rotting plank walls, but its dilapidated state served to camouflage it against the thick underbrush. Thinking the shack was empty, for no smoke rose from the chimney, Abel was caught off guard by the sharp crack of a rifle and the whine of a bullet zipping by.

"Hold your fire, it's me Abel!" he shouted, throwing up his hands.

"Abel?" called Logan, emerging from the open door. "What in blazes are you doing here?"

"I had some trouble on the river last night, and ended up near here so I thought I would stop by for some fresh duds and a bite to eat" said Abel, dropping his hands and approaching the shack.

"I had some trouble myself in Memphis yesterday, come on in and I'll tell you all about it."

The Beckwith brothers went into the old shack and Logan produced a half bottle of whiskey and some stale bread.

"Sorry I ain't got any coffee Abel, I didn't want to start a fire. Calloway's probably got posses everywhere looking for me" said Logan apologetically.

"What happened? Where are the boys?" inquired Abel.

"Calloway's got 'em all locked up in the calaboose down in Memphis. I hit the saloon and got the Marshal and his boys to follow me out of town. The boys were gonna hit the bank while they were gone. Everything was going smooth until I came around a corner and an old mule was sitting in the middle of the road. My horse threw me and before I knew it Calloway had caught up and had me dead to rights. We got back to town just in time to have the boys pinned as they came out of the bank."

"Why was there a mule in the road?" asked a puzzled Abel.

"Some hillbilly kid couldn't get him to move. It's all that durned kid's fault. I was gonna use that money to settle down with Flora. Now I imagine she'll take up with that senator. If that happens I'm going to find that kid and carve his liver for him" seethed Logan.

"Dang Logan, I'm sorry to hear about the boys. Do you think we could spring them if we hurried back to Memphis?"

"I ain't got time to worry about the boys right now; did you hear what I said about Flora? She's gonna marry that senator if I can't come up with enough cash to set her up right."

"Forget about that actress Logan," replied Abel "she's just stringing you along for all those presents you've been giving her."

"She is not! She loves me and I love her, now take that back!" shouted Logan, his frustration coming to a boil.

"All right Logan, settle down" said Abel trying to calm his volatile older brother "What about this kid, would you know him again if you saw him?"

"You're dang right I would, skinny kid wearing overalls, looks like he just came down from the mountains, he rides a worn out old mule and has the worst looking dog I've-" described Logan.

"Alouicious Rucker!" interrupted Abel.

Logan was shocked "Now how in the Sam Hill did you know that?" he asked.

"He caught me cheating at cards last night on a barge. They beat the hell out of me and threw me into the river a couple of miles upstream, that's why I'm in such sorry shape." explained Abel.

"How did that yokel catch you cheating? You must be slipping, little brother." admonished Logan.

"He's sharper than he looks." mumbled Abel, unwilling to relate the truth of his exposure.

"So you'll be coming with me to St. Louis then? Maybe we can get Flora to change her mind about running off with that senator and ruin that kid's day while we're at it" said Logan, his demeanor turning dark.

"I reckon I will." replied Abel.

Peabody Samuelson cursed his ill luck as he sensed the story of a lifetime slipping farther and farther away. He had wasted no time gaining passage on a steamer headed upriver, but after a little over a day's travel, the boat had run aground on one of the ever changing sandbars and so far the crew had been unable to budge the stuck vessel. Word had been sent back to Memphis for another steamer to come to the steamer's aid but until help arrived or the river rose there was nothing for Peabody to do but sit on deck with the rest of the passengers and wallow in self pity.

Some of the passengers sought relief from their boredom by hailing passing riverboats, and they eventually convinced the crew of a small barge carrying whiskey to come alongside and visit a spell. Drinking had never agreed with him, so Peabody declined offers to sip from the bottles which had been purchased from the traders and were being passed around the deck of the steamer, but his relentless curiosity drove the journalist to approach a member of the whiskey boat crew and inquire about news from upriver.

"Heard about a man that got caught cheating at cards by a dog" said the whiskey trader, who was a rough looking, bearded man enveloped in a heavy buffalo coat despite the humid warmth.

"A dog?" asked an incredulous Peabody.

"Yup, durndest thing I ever heard of. I guess the scoundrel was rat-holing high cards in his coat pocket and the dog spotted him and started raising hell. I never figured you could train a dog to spot a card cheat" mused the trader.

Amused, Peabody produced his pad and pencil and began to take notes. "When did this happen?" he asked, thinking if he could squeeze a quirky human (or canine) interest story out of the man the trip wouldn't be a total loss.

"Oh, night before last, I reckon. We passed them headed upriver yesterday. I saw the dog with my own eyes, kind of a queer looking mongrel."

"Who was the man who was caught cheating?" asked Peabody, anxious to glean any speck of truth from such an obviously tall tale.

"Fellow goes by the name of Abel Beckwith, though the way the story's spreading, he'll be lucky if he can ever show his face on the river again" said the boatman.

"Hmm, I wonder if he could be related to Logan Beckwith, the outlaw. He was captured in Memphis the other day you know" said Peabody, still scratching notes on his writing pad.

"Beckwith finally got caught? Now, that is a piece of news!" exclaimed the trader, "Who was it that finally stood up to that old bushwhacker?"

"Oh, a man named Alouicious Rucker subdued him and led the posse that captured the rest of the gang. I'm headed upriver to interview him for the Memphis Daily Appeal" said Peabody.

What a coincidence," said the trader

"Alouicious Rucker is the man who taught his dog to sniff out cheaters."

Peabody Samuelson's jaw and pencil simultaneously dropped at the startling revelation. "Rucker? You saw Alouicious Rucker?" shouted Peabody.

"Why sure I did." stammered the boatman confused by Peabody's outburst.

"What did he look like? Where was he going? Tell me everything!" urged Peabody, flipping his writing pad to a fresh page.

Initially caught on the back foot by Peabody's outburst, the whiskey trader recovered quickly at finding himself the center of attention of a genuine newspaper reporter, and settled in to supply the reporter with all the details he could recall. A trifling fact that he had never actually spoken to Alouicious Rucker wouldn't hinder him in the least.

Chapter 5

Mastering beasts as well as men, Alouicious Rucker proved to be the consummate animal handler, training his faithful hound to perform feats that men could scarce accomplish, and guiding his mighty steed with a firm, confident hand through places even goats would fear to tread. Wild or domestic, all beasts submitted to Rucker's iron will, and never before or since has any savage or stockman so completely subdued the animal kingdom.

--excerpt from "Al Rucker: a Western Legend" by Peabody Samuelson

Ruck stood at the rail of the river barge watching the slow dark waters of the Mississippi glide past. The trip upriver had been enjoyable, even a little idyllic, with clear skies occasionally punctuated by gentle spring rains which served to temper the afternoon heat. Thousands of migrating birds clouded the skies, while deer and other wildlife could be seen drinking from the river in the forested places between the sleepy communities dotting the riverbank. The camaraderie between the passengers which had developed after the exposure of the card cheat, grew as the days passed, with folks sharing stories, meals and drinks, enjoying the bond which only a shared adventure can bring. Thus, the captain's announcement that they would arrive in St. Louis early the next morning came as a bittersweet reminder that all things must pass.

The captain proved to be correct in his estimate, as shortly after dawn the next day the sparse settlements lining the riverbank began to come closer and closer together, finally merging into the bustling city of St. Louis. To Ruck, the city seemed to seethe with people scurrying hither and yon about their morning business. Not only the streets but as the barge came closer to the docks, the river itself became filled with watercraft of every size and description. Massive white steamers belched clouds of smoke into the air, stinking barges filled with heaping mounds of buffalo hides seemed to wallow in the water like the floating carcass of some massive beast and all the while, rowboats and canoes moved among the larger vessels like a pack of roving scavengers.

Arriving at the docks, the passengers on the barge prepared to disembark, gathering their belongings, and sharing heartfelt good-byes. Before leading Bolliver down the gangplank, Ruck asked the captain about the location of the nearest ferry as they had docked on the eastern shore of the river. He was relieved to find that there was a landing a short distance away, as he had no desire to linger among the noise and stink of the city which seemed to heave around him. Though uncomfortable in the crowded city, Ruck was conscious of the fact that after leaving St. Louis, it could be months before he had access to so much civilization again, so he availed himself of the opportunity, visiting a mercantile store to replenish his stores of traveling food, and having a farrier inspect Bolliver's shoes.

While Bolliver enjoyed a pedicure, Ruck and Whitey went to a nearby restaurant, for Ruck could foresee a dearth of hot meals in his near future. After many days of hardtack that tasted like saddle bags and the mediocre fish dishes available on the barge, the thick beef stew and slices of fresh bread tasted like ambrosia. With two heaping bowls and a multiple slices of bread to his credit Ruck finally pushed back from the table, feeling painfully full. Having paid with a ten dollar coin, Ruck tipped the waitress generously from the change she brought and headed toward the door. Ruck's mind was already focused on the next leg of his journey, so only Whitey noticed the man wearing a flamboyant off-white suit whose predatory gaze followed them as they walked out the door.

Jean-Batiste Le'Chiffre watched as the young man wearing overalls and his horrible looking dog left the restaurant, then quickly paid his bill and rose to follow. Jean-Batiste normally would have tried to have the waitress accept a worthless bauble or extend him credit, rather than pay actual money for his meal, but an ignorant hillbilly with a pocket full of gold eagles was an opportunity not to be missed. Brushing the crumbs from the lapel of his cream colored jacket with mauve piping, (which he mistakenly thought looked very dapper) Le'Chiffre rapidly made for the door and followed the young man at a discreet distance. Observing the young man as he collected his mule and paid the blacksmith, Jean-Batiste did not detect the desperate, fevered look of the average would be prospector, and rejected his "mining-claim grift" out of hand. No, the rube before him looked like a hayseed, and would therefore be more interested in land and livestock, so the "Cattleman Con" as he liked to call it, would probably be his best bet to relieve this turnip-merchant of his excess coin. Picking up his valise and surreptitiously following his mark, Le'Chiffre saw that the boy was headed for the ferryboat, the perfect place for what the con man had in mind.

As the ferryboat departed for the distant western bank of the river, Ruck was approached by a man wearing the worst suit he had ever seen. The cream colored affair with purplish piping and tie was topped by a matching top hat which made Ruck consider staying in St. Louis another day and taking in the circus this fellow apparently belonged to. The stranger was well groomed with wavy reddish-brown hair which fell to his shoulders, and an elegant, well trimmed mustache which suited his narrow features.

"Beautiful day isn't it?" said the man, speaking with a slight Cajun accent.

"It sure is" replied Ruck.

"My name is Jean-Batiste Le'Chiffre, and you look like a man who knows the land if you don't mind my saying so," said Le'Chiffre offering his hand.

"Pleased to meet you Mr. The Sheep. I'm Alouicious Rucker" said Ruck, shaking the man's hand politely.

"No, no, it's Le'Chiffre. With an 'L' and a 'C' and an 'R' at the end, it's French" corrected Jean-Batiste more than a little irritated.

"Sorry, I don't know much French" said Ruck, thinking maybe the man wore such ostentatious clothes to draw attention away from the worst name ever. "I just got to town, so I don't know much about the land around here either."

"Nonsense my boy, land is land everywhere you go, and I just so happen to have the opportunity of a lifetime for a man with a strong back and great vision such as yourself. You see I own a many acres of prime grazing land adjacent to the Kansas Pacific Railroad and find myself in need of liquid assets. It's my poor consumptive mother you see, the climate back in

France doesn't agree with her and I wish to transport her and her household out west where I hope the dry climate will relieve her suffering" said Le'Chiffre hardly seeming to take a breath during the diatribe. "I have the deed to one thousand acres of pasture land and four hundred head of cattle which I am willing to let go for a fraction of their worth. Yes, I fear that I have no choice but to make some lucky fellow into a rich cattle baron because of my mother's misfortune."

Buffeted by the verbal onslaught, Ruck struggled to make sense of the avalanche of words that threatened to engulf him, however he did manage to discern that somewhere amongst the muddle of French sounding words, the man had offered to sell him cows.

"I don't have much interest in raising beef," he said suppressing a shudder, "I'm just passing through on my way west."

Le'Chiffre was confused by the look of horror upon the young man's face, never suspecting that a grown man could have a dread of cattle, but without missing a beat, the charlatan changed his tack.

"West you say? Well by coincidence, I happen to moonlight as a railroad agent and happen to have access to discounted tickets for the westbound train which is leaving this very afternoon. I could let you have one for only forty dollars, which I might add is a substantial savings over the usual fare" Jean-Batiste offered in another stunning display of oral incontinence.

"Forty dollars?" exclaimed Ruck "I had no idea train tickets were so steep."

"My boy, a mere forty dollars is a pittance compared to the hardship you would suffer trying to overcome such a vast distance on your own, and the price includes a spot on the stock car for your fine mule here, and meals in the dining car for the duration of your trip. As I say it's a bargain compared to the depravation you would suffer crossing the Great American Desert, even on such a fine mount as you have here" spouted the con man, indicating Bolliver. The mule would have spit at the obvious lies the man was spewing if his mouth hadn't been so dry from eating too many oats at the blacksmith's place.

"I guess I'll take it then" said Ruck, thinking that forty dollars might be a cheap price to pay if it got the loquacious man to shut up. "You got the ticket with you then?"

"Oh no, not with me of course," said Le'Chiffre "just give me the money and I will meet you at the southern stock loading platform in a half an hour, we'll get your mule settled, and you'll be headed west before you know it."

"See you there then" said Ruck, handing over the money as the ferry docked on the west side of the river.

"Don't be late now!" said Le'Chiffre pocketing Ruck's money and striding purposefully away. It was not as much as he had hoped to con from the hillbilly, but all in all forty dollars was a tidy sum for less than an hour's work, a satisfied Jean-Batiste reflected, as he turned down the street in the opposite direction from the ticket booth.

Jean-Batiste's supply of fake mine deeds was currently running low and the money he had just conned from the rube on the ferry would be just what he needed to restock his valise with the fraudulent documents. Le'Chiffre tried to remember the name of the gambler who had provided him with excellent forgeries in the past, what was his name? Becker? Bosworth? No, Beckwith! Abel Beckwith! Yes, he would make inquiries about the whereabouts of Beckwith, who should be back in town again before long, if the gambler was still plying his trade on the riverboats, and use his new capital to get a fresh supply of fraudulent mine deeds which sold like hotcakes. Jean-Batiste began to whistle a tune as he strode down the boardwalk, thinking that the future looked as bright as ever.

Dale Honeyworth of the Brownlow Private Detective Agency stood concealed by the corner of a dry goods store and watched as Le'Chiffre whistled his way down the boardwalk. A tall lanky man in his middle forties, Honeyworth wore simple clothes of a common style and had imminently forgettable features which served him well in his capacity as a private detective. His sandy blonde hair was average length, and his regular features bore no distinguishing marks allowing him to blend easily with any crowd as long as it was comprised of mostly white people.

Honeyworth had been following the trail of the con man for weeks at the behest of the Kansas Pacific Railroad company, which had grown weary of the numerous outraged customers who were showing up at the railroad office waving all manner of fake train tickets and land grants, demanding to speak with the manager. Each of the victims had described a man in his thirties, with a Cajun or French accent, wearing a white suit who called himself 'The Sheep.' Tracing the whereabouts of a man so audacious as to wear a white suit and self apply such a silly nickname should have taken no great effort, but the con man had been tipped off by persons unknown about the detective agency's pursuit, and thus far had proved to be surprisingly elusive, giving Honeyworth the slip in cities and towns up and down the railroad line.

Honeyworth had his man now though, as two agents were positioned farther down the street, and in just a few short moments Jean-Batiste Le'Chiffre would be boxed in between them. After the con man had passed, Honeyworth stepped out from his position at the corner of the store and followed at an easy pace, not wanting to alert his quarry too soon. As Le'Chiffre drew closer to the jaws of the trap, Honeyworth quickened his pace, closing the distance between them to coincide with their approach to the other agent's positions. Too soon, one of the agents down the street broke cover and locked eyes with the charlatan. Betraying no surprise or hesitation, Le'Chiffre turned and broke into a sprint down an alley and out of the trap. Cursing, Honeywell ran after the man, and the other two agents took up the chase as well crying:

"Stop, The Sheep!"

Ruck found the railroad station easily enough, and after a few inquiries made his way to the stock loading area where he hoped to find Le'Chiffre with the promised train ticket. Finding an out of the way spot to wait, he watched as a train arrived and cowboys on horseback approached the cattle cars. Ruck grew uneasy as the sounds of the train subsided only to be replaced by the bellows of the confused and angry cattle packed into the cars.

Squatting down and scratching Whiteys shoulders as much to comfort himself as the dog, Ruck watched as a railroad man unlocked the cattle car and drew the door to the side. Steeling himself against the familiar terror he felt at the sight of milk cows he was used to, Ruck was totally unprepared for the sight of the monsters which emerged from the car. A tremendous set of horns appeared first, as wide as a man's outstretched arms and curling to vicious points which glinted in the noonday sun. The beast which followed was no less terrifying, having a narrow snout, wild eyes and skin that somehow seemed to hang loose on an emaciated body that appeared to be comprised of no more than bone and gristle. The Devil's own herd could not contain a more fearsome looking beast.

Ruck had almost convinced himself that he had seen no more than an anomaly, some sick, mutated, monstrosity which surely could not breed, but following the creature out of the cattle car came more of the things, each more terrible than the last. Pale to the gills and soaking in cold sweat, Ruck stood up and stopped a passerby:

"What is wrong with those cows?" he asked in a quavering voice.

Peering at the indicated cattle, the stranger gave a shrug, "Nothing that I can see, they look like perfectly healthy Texas longhorns to me." said the man, turning and going about his business.

As the cowboys moved the longhorns off the train, the confused and agitated cattle bumped and jostled each other, the clack of huge horns striking one another drove a chill down Ruck's spine and he was paralyzed with bowel-liquefying terror. Not only their appearance, but the demeanor of the beasts was vastly different than what Ruck was accustomed to from cows. The monsters seemed wild, and unused to the close proximity of men, and the cattle's eyes showed bloodshot whites as they rolled with anger and fear. The cowboys seemed to have difficulty controlling the roiling mass of stock, so it came as little surprise to Ruck, even as terrified as he was, when one of the horrible beasts broke the cordon of cow ponies and made its bid for freedom, bellowing in wild fury as it bore down upon him.

As Jean-Batiste zigzagged and doubled back through the city streets, he found himself back in the area of the railroad station. Being a gregarious man, Le'Chiffre had developed a good sized network of informants over the years, which had clued him in to the fact that a private detective named Honeyworth was trying to track him down for the railroad company. Being thus forewarned, Jean-Batiste had not hesitated to bolt when he saw two men who had the distinctive appearance and demeanor of undercover lawmen emerge from the alley into the street in front of him. Sprinting down streets and up alleys, Le'Chiffre took a circuitous route through St. Louis, heading for the depot, hoping to lose his pursuers in the snarl of traffic which surrounded the city hub.

Despite being capable of an impressive turn of speed, as well as sufficient agility to dodge around both wagons and pedestrians with ease, Jean-Batiste was betrayed by his own vanity as the white suit he wore served as a beacon to the men chasing him, flashing among the crowd like the raised tail of a startled deer. He increased his lead though as the pursuit neared the train depot, and Le'Chiffre knew that once he made it to the city's hub, he would be able to hide in any one of the numerous conveyances which constantly moved people and freight through the 'Gateway to the West.' Knowing that he must be out of his pursuer's sight before going to ground in a freight car or wagon, Jean-Batiste turned to look over his shoulder just as he rounded the corner near the stock platform into the path of the stampeding longhorn.

Panic seized Ruck, turning his prayer for deliverance into a high pitched, wordless shriek, as the enraged longhorn charged straight toward him. So awful was the cry, which Ruck figured would soon become his death-rattle, that the cow swerved around him at the last possible second directly into the path of a cream colored apparition which had just sprinted around the corner. Without breaking stride, the longhorn lowered its head and effortlessly, almost elegantly, lifted Le'Chiffre and threw him high into the air with a graceful toss of its horns. So high was Jean-Batiste thrown, that the longhorn was well on its way down the street before the man and his valise returned to the earth, the violent impact causing the case to open, scattering papers across the road.

Fearing the attack had been fatal, Ruck moved to see to the man who lay in a heap in the road, and was relieved to hear Le'Chiffre groan as Ruck turned him onto his back.

"Mr. The Sheep, can you hear me?" said Ruck, slapping the man lightly on the cheek.

"It's Le'Chiffre, you ignorant clod" mumbled Jean-Batiste, rousing slightly.

"It's a wonder you're alive," said Ruck "I thought you were done for."

Just then the three detectives rounded the corner coming to a skidding halt to avoid a collision with the horse of a cowboy who racing up the street to retrieve the stray longhorn. Seeing their quarry in an undignified heap in the middle of the street, the detectives quickly moved to encircle and restrain Le'Chiffre which took little effort since the con man was still quite stunned.

"Be careful with that man, he was just gored by a longhorn!" urged Ruck, objecting to the less than gentle manner in which the detectives had hefted Le'Chiffre to his feet. "What are you doing with him anyway?" he continued, "He's a railroad agent and an important cattleman in these parts."

"He's a wanted con man, and if you're taking his part, you must be one of his accomplices," Honeyworth said, drawing his pistol and leveling it at Ruck. "Put your hands up."

"Now wait a minute," said Ruck, slowly raising his hands, "What do you mean wanted? This fellow was meeting me here to give me train tickets, he's a railroad agent, just look at all those business papers that came out of his case." explained Ruck, nodding in the direction of the exploded valise.

"Joe, see what he's got there" Honeyworth ordered, still keeping Ruck covered with the revolver. One of the detectives complied, moving toward the mass of papers strewn about the street, while the other fitted handcuffs around Le'Chiffre's wrists.

The detective inventoried the assorted spilled papers as he gathered them. "Forged land deeds like the ones we found in Junction City, a few deeds for mines out west that I've never heard of, a license to practice medicine in Texas, a license to practice law in Georgia, a handful of fake train tickets, and what looks like the credentials of a Methodist preacher out of Maryland. That's about it, Dale." He said, shoving the documents back into the valise.

"That son of a gun cheated me out of forty dollars" exclaimed Ruck with dawning comprehension.

"You're lucky," replied Honeyworth, holstering his pistol, convinced that Ruck was innocent. "He took most people for much more than that. I'm Detective Dale Honeyworth, with the Brownlow Detective Agency; you had better come with us and give a statement."

"Yes, sir" replied Ruck. Relieved now that he longer seemed to be in imminent danger of being shot, arrested or gored by a rampaging longhorn, Ruck followed the detectives as they led Le'Chiffre through the streets of St. Louis, toward the city jail.

Chapter 6

Ever elusive and shrouded in mystery, Alouicious Rucker nevertheless left a mighty wake in his passing. Those who sought him whatever the reason, were continually caught up in the fervor caused by his passing, though continually thwarted in their attempts to contact, for good or for ill, the man himself.

--excerpt from "Al Rucker: a Western Legend" by Peabody Samuelson

Peabody Samuelson was miserable. The three days since the steamboat had been freed from the sandbar had arguably been the worst three days of his life. The weather was never comfortable, being either hot and disgustingly humid, or cold and rainy. The air teemed with hordes of mosquitoes so thick that one could hardly see. Not that there was anything to see anyway, as miles and miles of uninhabited shoreline passed with what was to Peabody almost unbearable tedium.

Surprisingly, the other passengers seemed to enjoy the regular sightings of deer, raccoons and the occasional snapping turtle, as if they had never seen such creatures before, but Peabody had no interest in the beasts which roamed the wild places. He took some solace in the thought that someday all of the chaos of the wooded low country which he passed through would someday be tamed, and replaced by the comforting sight of orderly civilization. The endless bugs and heat drove the bookish reporter to his cabin, but reading his notes and revising the story he was preparing for the paper made him seasick even though the motion of the riverboat was barely discernable. Thus betrayed by his weak belly, he was driven back to the rail and the fools assembled there who seemed to take some sort of pleasure from watching the dull landscape roll by.

After what seemed like an eternity to Peabody, the city of St. Louis finally came into sight. His relief at seeing the haze of industrial smoke hanging over the orderly buildings and hearing the myriad sounds of people going about their business on the docks and surrounding boats was palpable. Peabody looked forward to finding Alouicious Rucker, completing his interview and then spending a few days seeing the sights in the bustling metropolis. Therefore it was with great relief that he took up his bags and made his way down the gangplank and into the comforting embrace of the city.

He shortly found a hotel, where he got settled, bathed and changed into a fresh suit. Finally being free of the filth he had accumulated over the course of his journey through the wilderness, Peabody felt like a new man. Grabbing up the satchel in which he kept his notepad and writing utensils he whistled a jaunty tune as he left the hotel after getting directions from the man at the desk, and headed for the telegraph office to report his arrival in St. Louis to his boss back in Memphis.

The directions he received from the innkeeper were precise, and Peabody had no trouble finding the telegraph office, as he was used to negotiating his way through the warren of city streets. He sent Mr. Johnson a short message, explaining the lateness of his arrival in St. Louis, and inquired of the telegraph operator the latest news, for he felt that he had to have missed much, being cooped up on the riverboat for all this time.

"Most folks are talking about the jailbreak in Memphis, but I guess you know about that." said the elderly telegraph operator, whose name was Roy.

"Jail break? When did this happen?" said Peabody, aghast.

"Oh three or four days ago now I reckon." Roy surmised, "A stranger riding a big white stallion caught that Beckwith fellow that Marshal Calloway has been chasing for years, but Calloway held him for less than a day before he busted out of the calaboose and disappeared."

"Disappeared?" asked Peabody, drawing out his notepad.

"No one has seen hide nor hair of him since, even though they have every lawman in the area stirred up looking for him. Calloway even sent a message to the marshal here to have him be on the lookout, though if that outlaw is smart he will be halfway to Mexico by now," opined Roy.

"Where can I find your marshal?" asked the reporter, "I'd like to get a statement."

"His office is just down the street," said Roy, indicating the direction with a wave.

"Thanks," responded Peabody as he turned for the door. "Oh, one more thing," said the reporter, suddenly remembering why he was in St. Louis in the first place. "Have you heard of a man named Alouicious Rucker?"

"You mean the guy that taught his dog to play cards?" Roy responded with bemusement, "That story has been up and down the lines for days now."

"Thanks again," said Peabody, "You've been a great help." with that, he turned and headed out the door to find the marshal's office.

The telegraph operator's vague directions

proved to be surprisingly accurate and a short walk found Peabody entering the office of the St. Louis city marshal. The interior of the office was open and spacious, containing several desks, and the rear of the room was partitioned off with bars to form holding cells, only one of which was occupied at the moment. Peabody introduced himself to the deputy, who was a rotund man with a patchy red beard and thinning curly hair, and inquired after the whereabouts of the marshal.

Upon hearing that Peabody was a reporter, Deputy Billy Porter's face grew pale and he began to sweat. His boss the marshal disliked reporters and there was an unspoken order in the office not to give them any more information than what was required to get rid of the pests. On the other hand, reporters had a sneaky way of drawing information from Deputy Porter which he had never intended to divulge, causing his boss to reprimand him more than once. Thus caught between a rock and a hard place, the deputy entered the conversation with the hesitancy of a coyote investigating a morsel which might conceal a trap.

"Marshal Dunlop is meeting with the city council today," said the portly deputy, "he's likely to be there the rest of the afternoon."

Undeterred by the marshal's absence, Peabody readied his pad and pencil and asked the deputy: "May I inquire what actions, if any, this office plans to take to help find Logan Beckwith, who I hear escaped from the Memphis calaboose recently?"

"Oh, we'll keep an eye out I suppose," said the deputy cautiously, unwilling to make any definitive statements to a journalist "but we haven't heard he was coming this way. If he's smart he'll head for Mexico, or maybe the territories."

"Have you any information about Alouicious Rucker?" asked the reporter. "He's the man who captured Beckwith in the first place, and I have it on good authority that he at least was headed this way."

"Can't say as I have ever heard of the man" said the deputy, who did not keep up with the canine gambling circuit "Do you have a description of him?"

"Why yes," replied Peabody, flipping backwards through his notepad. "He would have to be a powerfully built man, as he subdued Beckwith with his bare hands, with dark hair and beard, riding a large white horse and accompanied by a dog that is by all accounts extremely intelligent."

A low chuckle came from the holding cells and a voice with a Cajun accent spoke up.

"That is the most inaccurate description of a man I have ever heard, unless there are two poor souls in the world burdened with the unlikely name of Alouicious Rucker. You may as well search the skies for flying pigs as search for Rucker using that description, as you will surely come across the porcine aviators first" said the prisoner, a slick looking man wearing a dusty cream colored suit.

"Quiet down there, Le'Chiffre!" shouted Porter, "no one is talking to you."

"Now wait a minute," interjected Peabody, "are you saying that you have seen Alouicious Rucker?" he said addressing himself to the prisoner.

"Alas, he was witness to the turn of grim luck that landed me in the confines of this cell" replied Le'Chiffre, in his inimitably loquacious manner.

"Why is this man here?" Peabody asked the deputy.

"He was brought in yesterday by some private detectives. He's been conning people out of money up and down the railroad lines for some time now" Billy replied.

"And what role did Alouicious Rucker play in this fellow's capture?" asked the reporter, turning to a fresh page in his notebook and writing furiously.

"None that I know of, but I was out when they brought him in, so you'll have to ask the detectives over at the Brownlow Agency" responded the deputy.

"Can you direct me to their offices?" pleaded

Peabody.

"Why sure, I'll draw you a map" said Deputy Porter, eager to deflect the journalist's attention onto someone else and avoid the wrath of his boss. "Ask for Detective Honeyworth, he's the one who brought this one in."

Peabody quickly thanked the deputy and left, heading straight for the Brownlow offices, thrilled once again to be hot on the trail of the heroic Rucker.

Following the deputy's directions, Peabody quickly located the simple sign proclaiming the Brownlow Detective Agency, and wasted no time in entering the offices. Upon entering, Peabody found the offices to be well appointed if not lavish with many desks filling the ample space of the room. He was greeted by a friendly man from behind one of the foremost desks who after Peabody had inquired about the individual in charge of the Le'Chiffre case, escorted him to the adjoining office of Dale Honeyworth.

"Peabody Samuelson, reporter for the Memphis Daily Appeal" said Peabody offering his hand.

"Dale Honeyworth. What can I do for you, Mr. Samuelson?" asked the tall yet otherwise nondescript detective, shaking hands warmly.

"I understand you were the one who apprehended the con man named Le'Chiffre who is currently in the city jail" Peabody said.

"Yes, my team and I caught up with him just a few blocks from here near the stock loading platform at the train yard. Are you doing a story on Le'Chiffre? I was not aware that his activities had carried him as far south as Memphis."

"Actually, I'm trying to find a man who I hear might have assisted in the apprehension. Alouicious Rucker is his name. He caught Logan Beckwith down in Memphis, and I've been trying to catch up to him ever since. I need a statement from him for a story I'm writing" Peabody explained.

"Rucker was there when we caught Le'Chiffre to be sure, but I wouldn't say that he assisted in the apprehension in any way. Le'Chiffre had conned Rucker out of forty dollars right before we made our move and was fleeing from us when he was gored by a runaway longhorn. Rucker was next to Le'Chiffre, trying to revive him when we caught up, but Rucker assured me it was only happenstance that he was there when he was." said Honeyworth.

"So shortly after Le'Chiffre conned Alouicious, he was gored by a cow?" asked the reporter, as he scribed notes. "Did you see Le'Chiffre get run down by the cow? What was Rucker doing at the time?"

"Well, Le'Chiffre was already lying in a heap in the street when my team and I came around the corner, so we weren't witnesses to the actual event, but from the testimony of Ruck and Le'Chiffre, those are the facts as best we can tell."

"Isn't it suspicious that after Rucker was conned, that the con man was found lying at the feet of his victim, himself the victim of a terrible accident? Such huge coincidence strains credulity" said Peabody, wondering at the obtuseness of a man who would not come to the conclusion that such a heroic figure as Alouicious Rucker had not had some hand in the downfall of the con man.

Having a vision of Rucker which was much more true to life, Honeyworth had no trouble believing that the guileless hayseed had not only been outwitted by the slick Le'Chiffre, but had also simply been in position to see the con man take a bad spill simply by accident. "What are you implying, Mr. Samuelson?" asked the detective, "That Rucker set some kind of trap for Le'Chiffre? That he knew that Le'Chiffre would be coming down the street in just that spot and drove a maddened cow into his path?"

"That sounds much more like the Alouicious Rucker I have heard about. He certainly has a way with animals. Did you know he taught his dog to spot people cheating at cards?" said Peabody, underlining the phrase 'set a trap' in his notebook.

Honeyworth, who had seen Whitey, was taken

aback at the thought the dog could be taught to do more than stink and maybe make children cry. "I'm not sure we're talking about the same Alouicious Rucker" hazarded the detective.

"Could there be two men traveling his direction with such a name? I hardly think so" said Peabody, "Where is Rucker now? I need to find him before he leaves to go out west."

"You missed him, Mr. Samuelson," replied Honeyworth, "The Kansas Pacific Railroad was grateful for his assistance in the investigation and awarded him free tickets to Las Animas, Colorado. He left yesterday evening."

Peabody slumped in his chair. The story of his lifetime would suffer greatly without a firsthand description of events by its protagonist. A broken hearted and dejected Peabody Samuelson thanked the detective for his help, made his way to the telegraph office and sent what he thought would be the final chapter of the story to Mr. Johnson back in Memphis.

Rising early the next day, still depressed about missing a key piece of his grand opus, Peabody packed his luggage and made ready to make his way back home in defeat. On his way to the docks, he stopped by the telegraph office to send word of his imminent return ahead to Memphis, and was surprised to find a message for him from his editor.

Rucker saga a hit. STOP. Keep it coming. STOP. Go west and interview Rucker at all costs. STOP. All expenses paid. STOP. No whiskey or sporting women. FULL STOP.

A roil of emotions engulfed Peabody as he read the telegraph message. The story of a lifetime was within his grasp once again, but to get it he would have to travel far beyond his beloved civilization for who knows how long. Determination won out over trepidation as Peabody asked the telegraph operator:

"Can you direct me to the train depot?"

Chapter 7

Alouicious Rucker, the hero who captured the dastardly Logan Beckwith last week, struck another blow for justice recently, this time in St. Louis. It has been reported that Rucker was instrumental in assisting the Pinkerton Detective agency in apprehending a con man going by the name of Jean-Batiste Le'Chiffre who had evaded capture for many months. Dale Honeyworth, the detective in charge of the case was quoted as saying "Rucker set some kind of trap for the con man" giving credit to Alouicious Rucker for removing yet another criminal from the streets.

--excerpt from The Memphis Daily Appeal
March 17, 1875

Logan Beckwith crumpled the newspaper in a fury, and hurled it into the small fire which was struggling to stay lit in the drizzling rain.

"When I catch up to that Rucker he's going to wish he had never been born." Logan said to his brother who was crouched across the fire with his hat pulled low against the rain.

Abel Beckwith was already wishing he had not been born as the journey from the hideout toward St. Louis had been miserable indeed. The two outlaws had relieved some sharecroppers of their horses, and rode north through the lowlands, traveling at night and avoiding the road as posses were sure to be searching for Logan. Coupled with the rain and mosquitoes, Logan's mood served to make the journey one of the most tense and unpleasant that Abel could remember.

Logan seemed not to notice any discomfort, or indeed anything at all as they rode, and any topic of conversation was invariably steered by Logan toward his worry about Flora and his hatred for Alouicious Rucker. Abel understood his brother's fear of losing his beloved Flora, but Logan's anger at the hillbilly went far beyond what was reasonable for a man who had been the victim of a run of bad luck, drifting into the realm of obsession. Veteran gambler that he was, Abel didn't feel the sting of wounded pride as keenly as his brother did, being long used to the capricious swings of fortune.

"St. Louis is a big place, Logan. How are we going to find Rucker? And what if he leaves before we can get him? Maybe we should just gather up Flora and head for Texas or Mexico instead. Forget about that kid."

"Like hell we will!" Logan snapped, "That kid might have cost me my only chance to be with Flora when he got me thrown into the calaboose. Not to mention taking all your money. We'll spring this fellow Le'Chiffre from the jailhouse when we get to St. Louis, he'll tell us where the kid is whether he likes it or not."

Abel sighed in resignation. A jailbreak would only add to their notoriety, and might get them hung to boot, but he had known his brother too long to think Logan could be dissuaded from a course of action once he had convinced himself of its merits. Maybe Rucker would have disappeared by the time they reached St. Louis, Abel thought, as he pulled his blanket over him and tried to get some sleep.

Abel knew enough about women to know that Flora Calhoun never had any intention of settling down with a man like Logan, and the sooner his brother figured that out the better. Logan's heart would be broken and he would be miserable company for a while but once they were shut of that woman for good, the brothers could head for the Indian Territory where the law was sparse and overworked, and from there to Denver or Santa Fe to get a fresh start. The gambler thought it would be a workable plan if he could keep his brother from getting them killed first.

Shortly after dusk, Logan roused Abel from his slumber and the two saddled their stolen horses, continuing their muddy bug-infested journey. The rain had stopped at sundown and crickets chirped as a huge moon rose over the trees dappling the forest floor with shadows. Logan did not notice this as his mind was filled with visions of Flora and the life they might have had together had it not been for Rucker. Thoughts of vengeance against Rucker and a restoration of that romantic vision served to blind the outlaw to the aesthetics of his surroundings as he focused only on guiding his horse to the sure footing which would bring him ever closer to revenge.

Abel appreciated the beauty of the night, despite the poor company, but all things being equal he would have preferred to be at a card table, with the lights and smoke and women and all around excitement of the life he loved. He knew his exposure as a cheat had finished his career on the Mississippi but there were plenty of mining camps springing up out west where a man such as himself could make a comfortable living among the miners who had more money than gambling skill. Maybe springing Le'Chiffre was not such a bad idea, Abel thought as he rode. He had played cards with the man before, and knew him to be a canny opponent. Abel had often toyed with the idea of heading west as the mining camps seemed to be a fruit ripe for plucking, and with a partner such as Jean-Batiste they could really clean up. Buoyed by the thought, Abel turned his attention back to his brother who was riding silently ahead of him. Yes, tagging along with Logan could work out well if he played his cards right, and Abel Beckwith always played his cards right.

The Beckwith brothers approached St. Louis under the cover of darkness. Wending their way through back alleys and avoiding the brightly lit main roads, the two men soon approached the back of the theatre where Miss Flora Calhoun regularly performed. Abel held the horses while Logan approached the back door of the theatre and knocked. The door was soon opened by Buford who poked his bald head out into the night.

"Logan, what are you doing here?" I thought you would be halfway to Mexico by now" said the big man.

"I came to see Flora, is she in?" asked Logan desperately.

"Sorry Logan, she left for Pittsburg with Senator Bradley this morning" said Buford, hating to be the bearer of such bad tidings.

"Left? How could she leave with him? Isn't she still doing the show?" asked Logan.

"Flora quit the show and married the senator the day before yesterday," replied Buford, feeling truly sorry for the outlaw he had come to like.

"Married?" Logan whispered, stunned by the news.

"As soon as she heard you had been arrested, she had me take a note to Senator Bradley. I didn't read it but I can imagine what it must have said, because they were married the next day."

Logan was speechless, his shoulders slumped in defeat and he turned away from the door without another word, making his way toward Abel and the horses.

"What's wrong, Logan?" asked Abel seeing his brother's stricken expression.

"Let's go" said Logan curtly as he mounted his horse and charged off into the night, causing Abel to hurry to gain the saddle and follow.

Having spent some time in the city, the brothers knew their way around, and after inquiring about the whereabouts of Le'Chiffre from some of Abel's less than reputable acquaintances, the two men arrived outside the jailhouse in the wee hours of the morning. Logan was usually very meticulous in planning the various robberies he and his gang had committed over the years so when Abel asked his brother what the plan was for freeing Jean-Batiste, he was surprised to receive a curt 'we go in and get him' as a reply.

In truth, Logan's confidence had been shattered by his capture outside Memphis, and subsequent loss of Flora had driven him to the dark depths of despair from which some men never recovered. Logan's innate sense of superiority had never allowed him to expect that the law would catch up with him, so the shame of having been thwarted by a common hillbilly coupled with the pain of Flora's spurning, caused the fall of Logan's towering hubris to be an emotional cataclysm. Now, rather than playing a calculated game of cat and mouse with the law, Logan's emotional distress made him more direct, if not sloppy in his scheming. Therefore it was without pause or hesitation that Logan and Abel dismounted in front of the jailhouse, pulled their neckerchiefs over their noses to hide their faces, drew their guns and walked into the front door.

"Put your hands up, lawman!" ordered Logan, breaching the door violently and drawing a bead on the portly deputy who was the sole occupant of the office at such a late hour. Abel quickly followed his brother into the jailhouse and wasted no time locating Le'Chiffre, who was currently the only resident of the holding cells.

"Give us the keys, deputy, and this will all be over soon" growled Logan, his eyes narrowing dangerously.

Quickly weighing his meager pay against the two armed men before him, Deputy Porter wasted no time relinquishing the keys to Abel who opened the cell door as Logan relieved the deputy of his sidearm.

"Let's go, Le'Chiffre, unless you want to stay here." Abel said to a startled Jean-Batiste who was still confused and groggy from having been awoken from a deep sleep.

"Right you are, my good man, let me just retrieve my few effects, which the gentleman has been so kindly holding for me, and we can be on our way." responded Le'Chiffre, the pressing nature of the situation marginally dulling his loquaciousness.

Jean-Batiste quickly located his hat and valise as the brothers bound and gaggd the deputy locking him in the now vacant holding cell. The men then left the jail, and mounted their horses, with Le'Chiffre riding double behind Abel.

"I thank you gentlemen for the assistance, and I don't wish to appear ungrateful, but one has to wonder what prompted such kindness from two total strangers?" asked Jean-Batiste as they urged the horses into a trot and headed quickly out of town.

"We ain't exactly total strangers J.B.," said Abel, pulling his neckerchief off his face, "and it wasn't just charity, we need you to help us find a man."

"I will gladly offer any assistance I can, as long as you can get me out of this city and away from those dreadful detectives of the Brownlow Agency." offered Le'Chiffre.

"We need to find Alouicious Rucker," Logan said, "the paper said you ran afoul of him and we hoped you knew where he was."

"The hillbilly with the threadbare mule? Why on

earth would anyone want to find that hayseed?" asked an incredulous Le'Chiffre.

"We got a score to settle with him." Replied Logan simply.

"The railroad agent gave him free tickets to Colorado as a reward, though I don't see what he did to deserve such largesse, he must be halfway to there by now." supplied Jean-Batiste.

"Then we'll head west and track him from wherever he gets off the train. This place is too hot for the three of us now anyway." said Abel, the idea of heading for Colorado fitting in nicely with his plans to fleece the miners.

"The railroad men will be on the lookout for us, and there will be a posse on our trail before long." said Logan, "We'll get some fresh horses and head southwest. If we can make it through Missouri we'll be safe once we get into the territory."

Abel almost groaned aloud, the thought of an overland journey across the breadth of the Indian Territory was not a pleasant one, but he could see few other options, and in spite of his brother's faults, Logan had always found a way to keep them one step ahead of the law. Unless they ran afoul of another rube with a stubborn mule, he thought, chuckling silently to himself.

The three fugitives liberated fresh horses from a

barn on the outskirts of town and made it out of St. Louis without attracting attention. They moved swiftly through the night, and made a cold camp in an isolated copse just as dawn was breaking the horizon. Having evaded the law successfully for many years, Logan knew the odds of their escape improved with every mile they traveled west. The border regions were thinly populated relative to the area around St. Louis, and the people of rural Missouri were in no hurry to cooperate with the authorities, as they still held deep resentments about the bloody guerrilla warfare which had raged throughout the area during the war. This close to St. Louis, they still had to take great care in their movements, but Logan knew that each day they would be able to loosen up and travel faster in pursuit of his nemesis

Chapter 8

Alouicious seemed to grow in stature as he made his way across the great American Desert, the vast vistas and dry climate nourishing the hero in ways the civilized east never could. As if God had made the man specifically to tame the west, Alouicious came into his own as he moved farther and farther west.

--excerpt from "Al Rucker: a Western Legend" by Peabody Samuelson

During the train ride through Missouri Ruck was excited, constantly looking out the window at the freshly plowed fields and verdant pasture land that the train passed through on the way to Kansas City. Idyllic farms dotted the countryside and fresh spring rains brought forth the impossible green of the season's first growth. Switching trains in Kansas City that evening, he made sure Bolliver was comfortable and took his seat scratching Whitey behind the ears and watching the landscape roll past until night descended and he could see no more. Overexcited and enthusiastic about waking in a far green country as yet unpopulated, Ruck had difficulty getting to sleep, but in the wee hours of the morning he finally dozed, the distinctive yet comforting smell of Whitey soothing him with its familiarity.

Ruck was awakened by the scream of the train whistle after a restive night and hurriedly looked out the window, expecting to be awestricken by his first glimpse of the American West. The sight that greeted him was not what he expected as the train shuddered to a halt. Coarse, brown, dead-looking grass the likes of which he had only seen in Tennessee during the worst of winters covered the ground which was a featureless plain broken only by low shape of what appeared to be some sort of primitive domicile partially dug into the ground. Quickly he moved to the other side of the train car thinking he must be viewing and isolated patch of blighted earth only to be confronted by the exact sight he had seen from the first window, complete with hovel.

Thinking he was witness to some terrible tragedy, a distressed Ruck inquired of a nearby passenger: "What happened around here? Has there been some terrible drouth?"

Looking up from the pages of his Bible, the passenger glanced out the window unconcernedly. "It looks like it always does. This must be your first trip out west."

"Yes sir," replied Ruck, "I'm from Tennessee, on my way to the Arizona territory."

"Best get used to that sight then, kid," said the passenger not unkindly, "you'll be seeing plenty of it."

Ruck's fellow passenger proved correct, as the day wore on the train moved across the endless prairie, giving Ruck new definitions of the words 'vast,' and 'empty.' He had heard tales of the 'Great American Desert,' as it was called but he had disregarded most of the descriptions as hyperbole. Never had he contemplated such a huge empty place. Why would people come here? Ruck asked himself, what would they do for food, for water? Free or even cheap land was a temptation to be sure, but once people found out what kind of land was to be had surely this dismal place would remain forever uninhabited.

Then he saw it. In such a featureless expanse the eye would gravitate toward any variation and so the black line which emerged from behind an invisible fold in the land immediately grasped Ruck's attention and held it. A solid dark mass was drifting parallel to the tracks in the opposite direction the train was heading. Ruck was confused and somewhat frightened by what he saw, until the dark mass moved closer, resolving itself into a massive herd of buffalo thundering across the plains. Almer had spun yarns about the great buffalo herds during their long talks in the evening, but he had assumed the old man's description of the size and majesty of the great buffalo herds to be greatly exaggerated. He had imagined large herds of large animals to be sure, but the sight which greeted him from the window of the train defied belief. The roiling mass of black and brown animals streamed by like a flood, and the rumble of their hooves rivaled, and then drowned out the sound of the train as it rattled down the tracks.

Ruck was captivated by the awesome sight, and oblivious to what was happening in the train car, so he was startled by the sound of gunfire which suddenly erupted around him. Expecting to find train robbers or marauding Indians Ruck chuckled in relief to find his fellow passengers all at the windows and firing guns of every description at the herd. Men, women, even a couple young boys fired rifles and pistols wildly in the general direction of the buffalo laughing as the sport provided a pleasant break in the monotony of the trip. Ruck readied his rifle, preparing to take a few pot shots at the massive beasts himself but held back as men on horseback came thundering into view, blocking his shot. Riding at a gallop along side the herd, men dressed in rough clothing of varying descriptions fired repeatedly into the stampeding swarm of buffalo. Unlike the wild shots of the passengers, the buffalo hunters' bullets felled one of the beasts more often than not, the huge animals falling to the ground to be trampled by those behind. The panicked buffalo tried in vain to escape their pursuers but the press of so many beasts could not be easily or quickly turned, and so the herd had little choice but to race ahead being picked off one by one by the hunters.

Soon the train moved out of sight of the stampeding buffalo and the hunters who followed them, leaving only the massive black forms of felled beasts dotting the prairie in their wake. Ruck was stunned at the number of dead buffalo that were scattered about the plains, and as the miles rolled by, the black carcasses turned to red as the train came upon the skinning teams, hauling wagons filled with buffalo hides, and soon even the wagons were left behind leaving mile after mile of prairie filled with meat left to rot. Ruck looked in wonder at the waste, as many in the south still struggled to feed their families only a few days of travel by rail away.

Many a night, young Ruck had lay awake imagining the great buffalo hunts he had heard described by Almer. He had been enraptured by the thought of the racing horses, the rumble of hooves, and the thrill of bringing a mighty beast down. But growing up with little, having to do without so much, he had never dreamed of such reckless squandering of such a great resource. Turning away from the window, he scratched Whitey behind the ears to comfort the dog, who had grown restive with the smell of so much blood in the air, and to comfort himself as a small part of his youthful illusions crumbled to dust.

Peabody Samuelson reluctantly boarded the train in St. Louis, ready to follow Alouicious Rucker west but having great misgivings about leaving civilization to trek across the wild hinterlands of the west. Peabody knew that the railroad would take Rucker as far as Las Animas, Colorado, but Rucker's ultimate destination seemed to be the silver fields of the Arizona Territory. Peabody had missed the train which left on the day he received orders from his editor to follow Rucker and was therefore another full day behind the man he sought. The reporter despaired of catching up to Rucker before the man struck out over land to a region where the conflict between the U.S. Army and the Apache still raged, and he feared that he may have to tread that dangerous path himself before he completed the assignment.

Peabody took his seat as the train moved slowly out of St. Louis. He clutched his valise tightly as his sight took in what he was sure was to be his last sight of civilization for some time. Traveling through Missouri, he tried to commit to memory the sight of the settlements and farmsteads lining the railway, wanting to have a clear vision of somewhere green to hold onto as he traveled through the vast desert to which he was bound. As a newspaperman, Peabody had read the reports of government surveyors, railroad officials, and returning Army officers which described the country west of the Missouri River as a desolate wasteland, unfit for habitation by anyone other than the primitive savages who lived there, eking out a living from the barren land. His trepidation only grew as he switched trains in Kansas City, leaving the Missouri Pacific railway behind him. This close to the river, the land was still fecund, but Peabody took the opportunity to purchase three canteens from a general store, and filled them as an emergency water supply.

As he made his way to his seat on the train, fumbling with his valise and canteens, he noticed a young woman sitting with an older man across the aisle from the seat he had claimed. She was plainly dressed with an unremarkable bespectacled face, and wore her brown hair uncovered and pulled into a rather severe bun. The older gentlemen who accompanied her looked much less refined, wearing well worn pants and shirt, a sweat stained hat, and several days' growth of salt and pepper beard. It wasn't the appearance of the pair which caught Peabody's attention however; it was the subject of their conversation which he accidentally overheard.

"It says here that the man set a trap for the rogue, causing a longhorn cow to knock the man down, allowing the Brownlow Detectives to capture him," said the woman.

"Folderol!" exclaimed the man sitting next to her "There's not a man alive who could teach a Texas longhorn to do anything on command, recalcitrant beasts that they are."

"But this seems to be a rather singular individual," continued the woman, "Remember, he is the one who taught his dog to play poker."

"I guess you can't believe everything you read in the paper," said the man gruffly.

"Excuse me," interjected Peabody, "I couldn't help but overhear your conversation, and I assure you that the events you are reading about were confirmed by actual eyewitnesses."

"And how would you know that?" asked the man, turning his baleful gaze on the reporter.

"Because I interviewed those eyewitnesses and wrote the story," replied Peabody a little defensively "Allow me to introduce myself. I'm Peabody Samuelson, reporter for the Memphis Daily Appeal."

"Pleased to meet you, Mr. Samuelson, my name is Eunice McCall, and this is my chaperone Buster Stewart," said the young woman "Don't mind Buster, too much time on the range has somewhat stunted his sense of decorum."

"The pleasure is all mine, Miss McCall, and I understand how you feel, Mr. Stewart, I know that I would never believe the stories about Alouicious Rucker if I hadn't followed the man for so long and investigated the stories for myself," said Peabody graciously, doffing his hat to Eunice and shaking Buster's hand warmly, "He truly is a singular individual, as Miss McCall so keenly observed."

"What is Mr. Rucker like in person?" asked Eunice, "I find it hard to imagine a man who so casually subdues outlaws and has such mastery over animals."

"Well, I don't know really," Peabody replied with regret, "ever since he captured Logan Beckwith in Memphis, I've been trying to catch up with him for an interview, but he simply travels too fast. I always arrive one day too late, just in time to hear of some amazing feat, before I race off to his next known destination. That's why I'm traveling west, you see, he boarded the train for Las Animas, Colorado, yesterday where I hope to find him."

"Why what a coincidence," exclaimed Eunice "Las Animas is our destination too. My uncle's ranch is in Cimarron in the New Mexico Territory. He has graciously agreed to take me in as my parents recently passed away."

"I'm sorry for your loss, Miss," said Peabody "I hope the western life agrees with you." At that moment, the picture of the west which Peabody had held in his mind's eye for so long was forever altered, as a place which played host to such an intelligent and respectable woman as Eunice McCall could not be all bad.

Over the course of the journey, Peabody and

Eunice became fast friends, discussing current events, and pointing out the various sights they saw as they traveled deeper into the arid plains. Even Buster loosened up as it became clear that Peabody was a gentleman, pointing out antelope and distant herds of buffalo far out on the prairie. Shortly after lunch on the first day, a heavy rainstorm swept across the plains, showering the parched land and tempering the heat which had begun to encroach on the railcar. The smell of freshly fallen rain on a dry land coupled with the cool pleasant breeze and even more pleasant company made the train journey across Kansas an enjoyable one for Peabody. The trip which the reporter had so dreaded when he boarded the train seemed to come to a close far too quickly for Peabody's tastes and it was with no small lamentation that he discovered the very next stop was Las Animas, and he would have to part ways with his newfound friends.

"I must say that this has been a surprisingly pleasant journey, thanks in no small part to you two," said Peabody as the train drew to a stop.

"I agree sir, the last two days seemed to just fly by," replied Eunice blushing prettily.

Seeing what was transpiring, Buster quickly stood up and grasped Eunice's baggage hoping to exit the train before the uncomfortable conversation progressed any farther, but he was far too late to stop what was happening between the young people and he almost groaned aloud when he noticed that the reporter was bolstering his courage to ask a difficult question.

"I hope you don't think less of me for being so forthright, but the thought of never seeing you again is a difficult one for me," stammered Peabody, who was visibly trembling with nervousness. "I wonder if I might ask your uncle if I could call on you once my assignment is finished?"

Buster closed his eyes and let out a weary breath at the blurted question. Buster's boss had given him the task of chaperoning Miss Eunice to the ranch, a simple task on the face of it, but now she had a prospective suitor, and Buster was sure he had just earned himself the privilege of every onerous, degrading task on the ranch for the foreseeable future.

"You can ask him if you like," replied Eunice nervously, trying in vain to hide behind her glasses. "Just ask for the McCall ranch; it's well known."

With that, Peabody doffed his hat, shook Buster's hand, and bolted for the exit. Eager to escape the uncomfortable situation but elated at the thought of formally courting Eunice, Peabody emerged from the train giddy with excitement as so far his adventure into the west had been easily the greatest time of his life.

Chapter 9

Notorious outlaw Logan Beckwith remains at large despite a massive manhunt orchestrated by U.S. Marshals in conjunction with local authorities. Lawmen throughout the south and even as far away as St. Louis have been told to be on the lookout for the villain ever since he made a daring escape from the Memphis city jail last week.

--excerpt from The Memphis Daily Appeal
March 23, 1875

Abel Beckwith couldn't imagine how his brother had lived like this all these years. The journey through Missouri had been fraught with tension as the three men had made their way across the state traveling only at night, hiding in abandoned barns or muddy creek bottoms during the day, always on the lookout for anyone, law or civilian who might spot them. Thus it was an exhausted trio who circled south of Baxter Springs and finally made it into the dubious safety of the Indian Territory. The fugitives had acquired fresh horses close to the Missouri state line and turned their newly liberated steeds west, angling a little south to avoid any over enthusiastic posse which might cross the border from Kansas.

Logan's energy seemed endless, even after days of catching only short naps in the roughest conditions and nights of riding quickly, almost recklessly through the darkness. His single minded determination to mete out justice on the agent of his downfall lent him a cold fury which fueled him during the arduous journey. Abel and Jean-Batiste however were not quite so consumed with thoughts of vengeance, and the brutal pace set by Logan had worn them to a frazzle. Abel thought that after having crossed into the Indian Territory where law was scarce, the men might be able to rest for a day and recover their strength before heading across the vast hostile territory which lay before them and said as much to his brother. Logan would hear none of it though as he pushed on long after the break of dawn for the first time since leaving St. Louis.

Jean-Batiste also had difficulty with the relentless pace, being a man more used to the relative comfort of a railcar, the miles of endless travel by horseback punctuated by brief naps on the ground had battered and stiffened his body to a point from which he feared he would never recover. Most distressing to Le'Chiffre though, was the fact that the fugitives' flight through Missouri had completely ruined his beloved suit. Crossing numerous creeks and sleeping on the wet ground had dappled his once cream colored outfit with so many various shades and consistencies of mud that he could scarce recall its original hue.

"When do you think we might stop for a rest?" Jean-Batiste inquired of Abel, his weariness and distress over his ruined clothes conspiring to curb his loquaciousness for once.

"Precious few places worth stopping at around here," replied Abel "but maybe we'll come across an outpost or roadhouse. We'll need supplies before long."

"I'll need a set of clothing more suited to travel if we intend to continue this primitive style of living, yet I have no money to pay for such, as the detectives confiscated all of my funds as evidence back in St. Louis," said Le'Chiffre, his mouth regaining steam quickly after a slow start.

"You won't need money," said Abel pitching his voice low to keep Logan from hearing "my brother is allergic to paying for anything he can just take instead. We do need to get you a pistol though. Anytime you're with Logan you end up needing one sooner or later."

"I'm afraid I don't have much aptitude in the use of firearms, I'm not in the habit of carrying one as it puts people on guard you see, and that is rarely conducive to the successful conclusion of a business transaction" explained Jean-Batiste as the verbal floodgates eased open promising a forthcoming torrent of language.

"We'll try to find you a scatter gun and stick you out front in case of a shooting scrape," teased Abel "that'll level the playing field."

"Quiet down you two!" snapped Logan drawing his horse up short "there's something yonder."

Looking ahead, the men could make out a thin column of smoke, barely visible against the low hanging clouds, emerging from a thicket of trees a few hundred yards distant.

"Well Abel, lets go get those supplies you mentioned," said Logan darkly, checking the load in his pistol "but I reckon that rest break will have to wait awhile yet. Le'Chiffre, you hang back since you ain't got an iron, and keep your head down, I'd also take off that top hat unless you want it shot off."

Jean-Batiste quickly doffed his conspicuous headgear and trailed after the brothers as they made their way toward the tree line. Entering the wooded area, the men dismounted and Le'Chiffre held the horses as Abel and Logan approached the source of the smoke on foot. A short distance into the woods, a small encampment was revealed, with two men seated on small barrels near a fire and a wagon parked a short distance away. The two men were armed, but not extremely vigilant, and as the brothers remained unseen as they moved in a half crouch toward the camp. Abel was prepared to hail the men, but stopped as he saw Logan draw his pistol and cock the hammer.

"Whiskey traders," mouthed Logan silently "you have the one on the right."

Abel nodded, drawing his pistol, preparing to defend himself if the traders grew jumpy and fired upon them. It was illegal to sell whiskey or firearms to the Indians populating the territory which naturally produced a booming black market. Such men were relatively common in the area and usually harmless, but when dealing with anyone in a region where law was scarce it always paid to be ready for anything.

Keeping low, the brothers made their way toward the camp, remaining concealed by trees and brush as best they could until there was no more cover to be had. Abel let Logan take the lead, as this was more his area of expertise, expecting his brother to hail the camp any time. Therefore Abel's surprise was complete when Logan simply stood, pointed his pistol and shot one of the traders dead. Shock caused Abel to hesitate and before he could even stand and take aim, Logan's second shot blazed forth, felling the second man as he rose.

"Boy you're as slow as molasses," said Logan crouching back behind the bush and looking over to make sure the traders had no unseen partners "all that card playing has made you soft."

"I thought we would palaver," said Abel still

stunned at the bloody turn of events.

"Why, do you have something to trade those men for the supplies we need?" asked Logan "I sure as hell don't."

Being fairly certain the camp was now empty, the brothers broke cover and took stock of the spoils. The whiskey traders must have recently entered the territory as they had been well supplied, having stores of food, blankets and plenty of ammunition in addition to numerous barrels of whiskey and several poor quality rifles, most of which Abel judged to be older than himself. Sending Abel to retrieve Jean-Batiste, Logan found a spade among the whiskey trader's supplies and shoveled moist earth over the fire so that no others would be drawn to the smoke as they had.

Returning shortly with Le'Chiffre and the horses, Abel quickly set about gathering supplies, wanting to be away from the grisly sight of the two dead traders as quickly as possible. Jean-Batiste stopped short and gaped at the sight of the corpses even though Abel had told him what had transpired at the camp. Le'Chiffre recovered quickly, but for once found himself lacking much to say as he secured an outfit more suited to traveling (though far less stylish) and sadly rid himself of his beloved cream colored suit. Abel handed Jean-Batiste a short, double barreled shotgun he had found on the wagon, as Logan inspected the horses which the traders had evidently used to pull their wagon. Finding the beasts satisfactory at least for packing or for trade later, the three men loaded their horses with necessities for the trip and rode away from the grim sight of the raided camp. Abel and Jean-Batiste felt subdued and rode in silence, but as a drizzling rain began to fall, Logan began whistling a low mournful tune, his mood improving for the first time since they had left St. Louis.

After days of traveling through the Indian Territory, avoiding any settlements or people they had seen, the three outlaws stood on a rise above an unknown river looking west across the shallow stream at land that looked flat, empty and dry as a bone.

"I've heard the plains were dry but that looks ridiculous," said an incredulous Abel "after we cross this river it could be a hundred miles to the next water."

"A hundred miles? Why we would never make it, no one could carry enough water to cross a hundred miles of land like that" lamented Jean-Batiste.

"Indians cross it all the time," said Logan.

"Yeah, but we ain't Indians," replied Abel.

"We ain't, but he sure is," said Logan, pointing down river at a lone figure approaching the river and kneeling to drink.

"Correct as usual Logan, but how does that help

us?" asked Le'Chiffre, afraid that the lone Indian man had just nominated himself to be the red-handed Logan's next victim.

"Boys, what we need is a guide, a scout like the army has," explained Logan, moving back from the rise and toward his horse "and I know someone who has just volunteered."

Kessay used his cupped hand to scoop the muddy water of the river to his lips. The day was hot, and he hoped to cover many more miles before bedding down for the night, so he drank deeply, to fortify his strength and clear his head for the long trek he had ahead of him. Kessay was a small man, slight of build and short, with the long slender limbs and red-brown skin typical of Apache people. His jet-black hair fell straight to his shoulders and was held back from his face by a red cloth tied around his forehead. Other than the headband, he wore only a breechclout with a small knife tucked into the waistband and tall shoes made of buffalo hide.

Sick of reservation life, Kessay had left the area of Camp Supply a few days before, and followed the north fork of the Canadian River west, heading toward his home in the far away White Mountains, near what the whites with their usual imaginative flair called 'Camp Apache.' He didn't consider himself a renegade, as he was only in the Territory by mistake. Kessay had been on his way home from a visit with his sweetheart, who lived on the nearby San Carlos reservation when he ran afoul of the filthy drunkard that passed for an Indian agent, and before he knew it he was clapped in irons and shipped halfway across the country to this ugly barren land.

Truth be told, Kessay didn't mind the arid scrubland so much because it reminded him of his sweetheart. Not that she was dry and prickly, but the area in which she lived, across the Black River from his own mountainous home, was sandy, brown, and comparatively flat, very similar to the miles of almost featureless plain he had already covered and the miles of the same he had yet to go.

Since leaving Camp Supply, Kessay had seen very few other people, and those had been groups of plains tribesmen or columns of cavalry far out across the prairie, so as he made his way through the canyon which the river had cut through the land, Kessay made the childish mistake of letting his mind drift toward thoughts of home, never imagining that there was another human being for miles around.

When the three horses topped the rise and headed straight for him, Kessay froze. He had only his small knife with him, which would be of no use against the three armed horsemen who spread out to encircle him as they negotiated the steep slope that formed this part of the canyon. To be caught by surprise like this was shameful for the Apache man, but with a little bit of guile maybe he could protect his people's fearsome reputation, sometimes white people could be made to believe anything.

Kessay stood still, affecting calm as he tried to ascertain who the men were, they seemed too sober to be comancheros or Indian agents, and they didn't have the ragged, wild look of army scouts either. The men had dark circles under their eyes and sunken cheeks, appearing as if they had gotten little rest or had been under stress for many days, their horses too kept their heads low and moved gracelessly, clearly exhausted. Kessay figured the men for fugitive outlaws then, as there were only a few reasons that three white men would be traveling up the Canadian River from the Territory and into no man's land. If they were fugitives, Kessay was in bad trouble, and he suspected that he would have to think quickly if he wanted to survive the next few minutes.

"It took you boys long enough; I was starting to think you would never catch up." Kessay said seizing the initiative before the lead rider could speak.

Caught off guard, Logan drew up his rein and leveled his rifle at Kessay, "What do you mean by that?" he asked.

"I've been waiting for you guys to catch up for a couple of days now, I was beginning to think the posse had caught you," replied Kessay, gambling that he had correctly estimated the men's reason for being in this forsaken place.

"I think you've got us confused with someone else, fella, we weren't planning on meeting anyone out here," said Logan.

"No, it's got to be you, I heard you were coming from my brother the coyote, and there's no one else around for at least fifty miles," said Kessay, silently praying that the whites were gullible enough to fall for such a colossal whopper.

"Do you know your way around here?" asked Abel, who was looking uneasy at the apparently prophetic Indian.

"Of course," Kessay lied smoothly, "Coyote told me you'd need help to cross El Llano and I was to help you, so the posse didn't get you."

"What posse?" growled Logan.

"Oh, they're a day or so behind you, but if we hurry, we'll be too deep into El Llano for them to catch up with us" as he said it Kessay knew he was on the right track as the men, rather than protesting innocence, glanced around as if to spot the fictitious posse. Or maybe not so fictitious? For all Kessay knew, there might be a real posse after these men, and if so he planned to be far away when they were caught.

"What is El Llano?" asked Jean-Batiste hesitantly pronouncing the Spanish words.

"You're at the edge of El Llano Estacado, no one ever makes it across El Llano if they don't know where the water is" explained Kessay deciding to season the web of lies he was spinning with a dash of truth. "Let me ride one of your extra horses, we had better get a move on if we're going to outrun that posse."

As the buffaloed men lowered their weapons and offered the reins of a remount to Kessay, the Apache knew he had them hooked. All except the Cajun though, as the man seemed to be trying to hide a knowing smile, Kessay knew he would have to watch him as they traveled west. This time of year, the spring runoff should have the Canadian River running strong, and one could probably simply follow it, having plenty of water available all the way into the New Mexico territory.The whites didn't know that however, and Kessay didn't feel inclined to clue them into the fact, for as long as the desperados thought they needed him, he might avoid being killed by the evil looking leader of the outlaws.

Being a consummate liar himself, Jean-Batiste was impressed by the huge load of road apples the Indian had served up, and instantly took a liking to the little man. Logan still appeared wary, but Abel had, to Le'Chiffre's surprise, apparently swallowed the whole outlandish story. As the Indian led the party back up to the top of the canyon and headed west into the setting sun, Jean-Batiste kept his thoughts to himself, unsure of how the ever more volatile Logan would react to being swindled so mightily.

Chapter 10

For someone born and raised in the cities of the east, tales of the west may elicit feelings of dread, or even fear at the seemingly endless list of hazards and hardships encountered by travelers to the region. Such was my experience, for as a newspaper reporter I was privy to stories of western adventures filled with such peril and woe as to make the listener scarce believe any normal human wouldn't last more than a day in such terrible environs. Let me assure you however, that such is not the case, as my initial sojourn west of the Mississippi proved to be one of the most pleasant and enjoyable of my life.

--excerpt from 'In Pursuit of a Legend, a Memoir' by Peabody Samuelson.

Despite the melancholy introspection brought on by witnessing the buffalo hunt, it was a lighthearted Ruck which exited the train in Las Animas, Colorado and took a deep breath of the thin, dry air which was so different from that he was used to in Tennessee. Bolliver seemed relieved to be finally leaving the train (though a little disappointed that the obnoxious Whitey had survived the trip) and the three were excited by the prospect of continuing their journey.

After being cooped up on the train for so long, Alouicious was glad to be out in the open again as he hastily made his way toward the general store to restock his supplies with Whitey running circles around Bolliver, jumping and barking in joy at being reunited with his playmate. The scenery around Las Animas was similar to the many miles of plains that they had journeyed through to get there, but the monotony was broken by the tree lined banks of the Arkansas River which cut a lazy path through the grasslands surrounding the village.

Arriving in front of the general store, Ruck hitched Bolliver to the post and made his way inside, Whitey elected to remain with Bolliver, incorrectly supposing that the mule would want company after his isolation during the rail journey. Replenishing his supply of jerky and hardtack, (which he was quickly becoming tired of) along with a few apples to break up the monotonous fare for both himself and Bolliver, Ruck asked the merchant about the condition of the road to Santa Fe.

"The road shouldn't be too bad this time of year," opined the shopkeeper, a balding, bespectacled man who enjoyed his occasional role as a travel consultant, "a little muddy maybe, but Old Bob hasn't complained much lately."

"Who is Old Bob?" asked Ruck.

"Old Bob and his nephew Josiah run the mail between here and Santa Fe. In fact, he just got in this morning if you want to ask him yourself. If he's not still at the train depot, he'll be across the street at the saloon."

The shopkeeper proved to be correct about the habits of the mail carrier, for when he arrived at the saloon and inquired about the whereabouts of Old Bob, the bartender nodded in the direction of a man with a grey beard which tumbled down his chest like a frozen waterfall and wearing clothes which had obviously seen many a mile.

"Pardon me sir, but are you the mail carrier?" asked Ruck.

"I'm *a* mail carrier," replied the man with a gap toothed smile, "but surely not the only one. My name is Robert Blackwell; most folks call me Old Bob. What can I do for you, sprout?"

"My name is Alouicious Rucker, but you can call me Ruck," said the younger man, put at ease by Old Bob's friendly manner "I'm headed toward Santa Fe, and was hoping you could tell me which road was best to take."

"Pleased to meet you, Ruck," said Old Bob shaking hands warmly, "What brings you to our little slice of the world?"

"Just passing through really, I'm headed for the Arizona territory and thought I might stop by the old pueblo on the way" replied Ruck, who had heard of the ancient Spanish settlement from Almer who had traded beaver pelts there in his years as a trapper.

"It's a sight worth seeing, sure enough" Old Bob said, "but some of the trails between here and there are sure to be rough going this time of year. The runoff plays hob with some of the mountain passes in the spring. I'll tell you what, unless you're in a hurry, you can ease along with me and my nephew, we're headed that direction in the morning with the mail that came off the train today."

"Many thanks Bob, I'll do just that," said Ruck, grateful to have a guide through unknown country. "Can I buy you another round?" he asked, indicating Old Bob's empty glass.

"Nossir, one is my limit," Old Bob said, "it's nice to wash down the trail dust, but strong drink is a mocker, as the Good Book says."

"Amen," agreed Ruck, heartened to meet such a kind, temperate soul.

Just before dawn the next morning, Ruck

emerged from his bedroll which he had spread beneath a tree on the banks of the Arkansas, and took in the peaceful Colorado morning. Even the usually energetic Whitey sat quietly listening to an isolated bird sing a tentative note or two, as if warming up for the performance to take place at sunrise. The crisp, dry air was perfectly still as if husbanding its strength for the strong gusts of spring wind which were sure to whip across the plains shortly after sunrise and the growing light brought the tranquil scenery into greater focus with every passing moment.

This was the west Ruck had been looking forward to since leaving Tennessee. The peace of a land which existed as God had made it, sparsely populated by men who were genuinely concerned with the welfare of their neighbors. Almer had often spoken to Ruck of a time long before the war, when goodwill and charity was the order of the day amongst the old timers. Almer had believed that the evil of slavery had brought God's wrath to the people of the south, and that the war was just the beginning of their trials, as the society which was rising from the ashes of the conflict was marked by a covetousness which not only affected the upper classes, but tainted the common folk as well. Ruck wasn't sure about this, as he had always been less philosophical than his old friend, but the kindness of the folks he had met since arriving in Colorado sat well with him, and assured Ruck that he had made the right choice in coming west.

Saddling Bolliver, and loading his few supplies, Ruck mounted the mule and headed toward his rendezvous with Old Bob. His timing was perfect, for as he arrived at the agreed place on the south side of town, he could see Old Bob and a younger man riding toward him. He was relieved to see that the men were mounted on smallish horses, as he had been worried that Bolliver would struggle to keep up with larger steeds.

"Good morning!" said Ruck enthusiastically.

"Good morning to you," replied Old Bob, "this here's my nephew Josiah, he's riding with me so he can learn the route and take a turn at the duty once in a while" the old man said indicating a heavyset young man with wavy blonde hair and beardless cheeks riding a slim paint pony.

"Pleased to know you, Josiah," said Ruck, nodding toward the young man "and thanks again for having me along."

"Think nothing of it, Ruck," said Old Bob, "it never hurts to have another set of eyes to be on the lookout for trouble. I've had good luck on this road so far, but one never knows in country like this."

"And it'll be nice to have someone else to talk to besides this old coot" joked Josiah, winking at Ruck and flashing a teasing grin at his uncle.

"You just don't recognize wisdom when you hear it," replied Old Bob affecting false bluster, "you could learn a lot from an old hand like me if you would just pay attention."

Ruck chuckled, amused at the exchange, and suddenly lamented that Almer had declined an invitation to come west with him. His old friend would have gotten along famously with Old Bob and his nephew.

"That's a fine looking mule you got there, but I don't guess I've ever seen a dog quite like that one" said Josiah noticing Whitey for the first time.

"This here's Bolliver and the dog's name is Whitey," said Ruck, patting the mule affectionately on the neck "Bolliver has been with me since I was just a kid, but Whitey took to following me around just after I left the Appalachians."

"Bob says you're headed to Arizona. You going to strike it rich in the silver fields?" teased Josiah.

Embarrassed Ruck replied: "I don't know much about mining I guess, but I thought I might give it a shot. I didn't have much else to do, so here I am."

"Well boys, we can jaw just as easily riding as we can sitting still, so we may as well get going" said Old Bob, clicking his tongue to get his horse moving.

The two young men urged their mounts to fall into step behind Old Bob's mare as Whitey, eager to be underway, gave a sharp bark and sprinted ahead of the men, pursuing adventure with the unfettered joy that only a cur can muster.

The slender cow ponies Old Bob and Josiah rode were deceptively quick and over the course of the first day over relatively flat land, the two men had to continually rein in their mounts to avoid leaving Ruck and Bolliver behind. But as the land rose, becoming more steep and rugged as they moved south, the sure footed, strong mule came into his own, more than matching the pace set by the longer legged horses. After the long journey by boat and train, Bolliver was happy to be again traveling under his own steam, comforted by the familiar weight of his friend. Bolliver's pleasure during the journey was only heightened by the fact that the horrible dog seemed too busy about his idiotic business to pester him.

With a surfeit of new sights and smells which required investigation, Whitey had no time for the frivolous games that he and the mule usually enjoyed. Squirrels, deer, and even a close encounter with a skunk provided Whitey with plenty to do since the dog considered it his righteous duty to make sure that all God's creatures knew that he was boss universal. Returning to check on the men for perhaps the fiftieth time that day, Whitey was preceded by the clear evidence of his confrontation with the skunk which had not been as one sided as he had imagined.

"Whew, that dog of yours must have got into it with a skunk," said Old Bob waving a hand ineffectually in front of his face "and here I thought the smell of that dog couldn't get any worse."

"I guess he showed you," replied Josiah, chuckling despite the burning stench.

"Get out of here Whitey," admonished a mortified Ruck, "go roll in a cow flop, maybe it'll take the edge off your stink."

Whitey assured himself that the men were doing just fine, having even invented a new game, (the point of which was apparently to make one's eyes water while trying to ride as far away from him as possible) and raced back into the brush beside the trail to continue his scouting mission. Glad that Ruck had finally come to his senses and run the awful cur off, Bolliver quickened his pace, trying to leave the dog's miasma behind them.

The weather was mostly clear as the men made their way toward Santa Fe, the forested country through which they traveled serving to dull the wind which Josiah assured Ruck blew almost continuously in the flatter parts of the region. Old Bob and Josiah amused Ruck with their playful bickering, harmlessly disagreeing and teasing one another about every subject which came up in the varied conversation. The men spent their days in the saddle commenting on the various aspects of the landscape they passed. Ruck asked many questions, the answers to which Old Bob and Josiah would initially disagree about, arguing in a light hearted fashion until the original query was lost in the forest of digressions the two men indulged. Despite this circuitous path of the conversation, Ruck learned much about the surrounding landscape from the two mail carriers who had spent much of their lives sojourning in the area.

During the evenings, around a small fire, the discussion turned to hearth and home, with Ruck regaling his friends with tales of Bolliver's many exploits and somewhat wistfully relating tales passed to him by his friend Almer. Thus when Old Bob informed Ruck that they would reach the pueblo of Santa Fe the following day, the news was bittersweet as the time had passed far too quickly.

The wranglers of the M-bar ranch were bone weary as they passed the outskirts of Santa Fe and turned the herd northeast. Their employer, Mr. McCall, had purchased five hundred head of Texas longhorn cattle from an outfit near Lincoln, New Mexico and driving the herd back to Cimarron had proved to be an unpleasant and difficult task.

Longhorns were notoriously ill tempered at the best of times, but these in particular had just been pulled from their winter range and the recalcitrant beasts gave new meaning to the phrase 'wild, wooly, and full of fleas.' Unused to even the proximity of men, much less trail broken, the cattle would constantly stray and straggle, seeming to take a malicious pleasure in defying the men who struggled to keep the herd together and pointed in the right direction, and double the normal number of men were required at night to keep the herd from splintering during the hours of darkness. The lean, tough, longhorns were energized by a few weeks of green springtime provender and the task of driving them was like driving a herd of deer. The cattle were alternately belligerent and panicky, one minute fleeing the cowboys and the next turning at bay giving the impression that they would fight to the last before being driven another step.

Thus it was an exhausted group of wranglers and their mounts who circled to the east of Santa Fe and struggled to turn the herd northeast at what was the approximate midpoint of their journey. It may have been wishful thinking on the part of the wranglers, but as the herd headed into the rolling uplands northeast of Santa Fe, the herd finally seemed to calm, trudging along placidly, giving the weary cowboys some respite from the constant opposition which the cattle had to this point provided. The calming of the herd soon caused the cowboys to relax, and after such a harrowing journey, it was but a short step from relaxation to drowsing in the saddle for many of the exhausted cowboys. It seemed that the longhorns could sense their captors reduced vigilance, and took the opportunity to engage in what could only be described as a bovine revolution.

The lead bull, which was a massive white beast with curling horns wider than the outstretched arms of a man, quickened his pace and the front rank of the herd behind him immediately followed suit. With a unity of purpose that the herd had yet to display to the cowboys, all five hundred head were soon trotting, and jostling together, gaining speed with each step. For the drowsy cowboys it seemed to happen instantly, one moment the herd was finally behaving itself moving along as it should, and the next moment a full fledged stampede was in progress. The wranglers responded as one, spurring their jaded horses toward the head of the streaming mass of longhorns in an attempt to stem the tide before the long legged cattle outdistanced the wranglers and disappeared into the hills.

Ruck and the mail carriers set an easy pace as they emerged from the hills into the flatter country surrounding Santa Fe. The men were jovial, telling jokes and stories to pass the time, but there was a subtle, subdued air over the group as they neared their destination, for each knew that their burgeoning friendship would soon be parted as Ruck went on to the Arizona territory. Whitey's skunk smell had diminished to the point where he was tolerable to be around, and only Bolliver seemed to object to the dog's presence.

The woodlands gave way to rolling grasslands and rocky bluffs, and Old Bob declared that soon the ancient Spanish pueblo of Santa Fe would be in sight. Low clouds turned the wide western sky a slate gray, promising the first rainstorm to mar the unbroken pleasant weather the men had been blessed with on the journey so far. Lightning flashed at various places across the plain, sometimes with visible bolts, sometimes only brightening the clouds without revealing itself. The sound of thunder was frequently heard, mostly rolling, sometimes cracking as a bolt struck close causing the men to increase their pace, hoping to make it to Santa Fe before the deluge began. The air grew moist, becoming fresh with the unmistakable smell of rain in the desert and Ruck began to see isolated raindrops strike the ground around him. The rolling of thunder increased, becoming almost steady as the men hurried across an arroyo already displaying a trickle of water which promised to become a torrent before long. Approaching the top of the rise beyond the gully, a slow steady rumble grew in pitch and volume causing Old Bob to rein in his pony and stare intently at the top of the rise.

"I don't think that's thunder," the old man said just as the maddened herd of stampeding longhorns crested the rise bearing down upon them.

Though the men were caught off guard, Bolliver and the two horses quickly sprang into action, bolting in three different directions. Too surprised to be horrified by the sight of the deadly herd, Ruck clung to the saddle horn as Bolliver turned to the left and made a valiant effort to show the rampaging cattle his heels. Ruck turned in the saddle just in time to see Old Bob disappear behind the embankment of the arroyo they had crossed, with the leading longhorns of the panicking herd hot on his heels; of Josiah there was no sign. He quickly turned back to the right just as the stampede overtook Bolliver. The faithful mule gave his utmost to escape the grisly fate which surely awaited them all, but in the end he was not fast enough, for as the streaming mass of cattle pressed around him Bolliver stumbled, falling to the ground and pitching Ruck from the saddle. Ruck hit the ground hard and something struck the back of his head, he didn't have time to wonder whether it was a rock or a hoof as blackness engulfed him.

Whitey found himself in a situation which was not a game for the first time in all his dog years, and ran flat out beside the mule, his ears held back and his nose stretched to the fore. Never given to overanalyzing a situation, Whitey simply ran. He could have outrun the mule fairly easily, but he held back, urging Bolliver to greater speed though his frantic barks were drowned out by the cacophony of the thundering hooves around them. Whitey knew that he and his friends were in trouble when the first cow drew abreast, and he began to seriously doubt that any of them would survive as more of the creatures came into view to either side. He kept Bolliver in view out of the corner of his eye, and when he saw the mule go down, Whitey immediately turned back and raced to the mule's aid.

Bolliver was stunned after falling, but wasted no time getting to his feet. His mild surprise at even gaining his feet was dwarfed by the surprise he felt at seeing Whitey, who was holding his ground in grim defiance of creatures many times his size, snapping and lunging at any of the rampaging cattle who came too near, creating a small area of safety behind him as the longhorns streamed around him. Bolliver made out the still form of Ruck lying on the ground near the dog, and the sight drove any thoughts of escape from his mind as he dove into the fray, rearing and lashing hooves at the stampeding cattle to widen the small gap that Whitey had created. The battle seemed to last an eternity for Whitey and Bolliver, as they struck against the enemies who threatened Ruck and suffered many blows in return, but soon the flow of cattle lessened, and the fog of war lifted in time for the mule and dog to notice the cowponies thundering past in pursuit of the wayward herd, their riders gazing at the battered pair in wonder.

Chapter 11

While pursuing a legend, if one was unsure of the whereabouts of Alouicious Rucker, one only had to wait, and listen, as surely it was only a matter of time before some bit of news about a feat of outrageous daring or heroism was heard and one could be sure that he had picked up the trail of the mighty Rucker again.

--excerpt from 'In Pursuit of a Legend, a Memoir' by Peabody Samuelson

Peabody sat at the desk in his hotel room trying, but failing to get any work done. After leaving the train, he had inquired around town trying to find anyone who had seen or spoken with Alouicious Rucker with no results. Las Animas was a small town, more of a village really, and it had only taken Peabody only a few hours to interview practically everyone in town, but no one could recall having seen anyone matching Rucker's description. Peabody had left word with everyone he spoke to that any news about Alouicious Rucker would be welcomed and rewarded if delivered to him at the hotel. According to his discussions with the railroad men back in St. Louis, the reporter knew that Rucker had only booked passage on the train as far as Las Animas, but it was as if the man had simply stepped off the train and disappeared. The only stranger that anyone could recall disembarking over the last few days had been an overall clad young man riding a mule who didn't match Peabody's mental image of Rucker at all. The man the reporter was supposed to interview had apparently vanished into the picturesque landscapes of the west.

The thought of the heroic figure riding off into the setting sun, fit nicely with what the reporter thought he knew about Alouicious Rucker so far, and Peabody was struck by the idea of turning his notes into a book. Eunice was well educated, and apparently had a love of literature to match his own, maybe she would look with greater favor on him if he was a published author, rather than just a humble reporter. Peabody was not so confident or ambitious as to imagine that he could pen some great epic, but a dime novel, even a series of dime novels would certainly be within his capabilities, and if his efforts bore fruit, it would only strengthen his position when he called upon Eunice at her uncle's ranch. Energized by the idea, Peabody purchased a new writing tablet from the general store and took a small room at the hotel and sat down to begin his work.

Despite the vast amount of notes he had compiled since first hearing about Rucker, Peabody had difficulty deciding where to begin. The blank page seemed ready to receive his eloquence, but every time Peabody began to organize an introductory thought, his vision of a great western hero wavered and his mind wandered to the train and the beautiful, intelligent woman he had met there. Frustrated at his inability to focus, Peabody rearranged his notes for perhaps the tenth time and sat up straight in his chair, in a feeble attempt to discipline his wandering mind.

He started at the beginning, reviewing the notes he had taken during his interview with Marshal Calloway in Memphis, Peabody rediscovered a small notation that indicated Rucker might have come from the Appalachian Mountains in Tennessee. Peabody had never been to the Appalachians but his mental image of them was of a hinterland, sparsely populated with unreconstructed hillbillies, he wished there was someone he could consult with to refine his fuzzy view of the region. 'I wonder if Eunice has ever been to the mountains?' he thought, 'I bet she would have some insight into the motivations of a man who was brought up in such a backwater.' After nearly an hour of such circular musings, Peabody looked down on the page to find only a crude doodle of the side of Eunice's face where her eyeglasses accented her cheek bones. Peabody let out an exasperated breath and lay his head on the desk.

"This is going to be harder than I thought," he said to himself.

Even after struggling with the blank page late into the night, Peabody woke at dawn, his eyes seeming to snap open as if spring loaded and refusing to close again. As he lay in the hotel bed, trying to get back to sleep, the thought of traveling to the McCall ranch and seeing Eunice insinuated its way into his sleep addled mind. As ideas of questionable wisdom are wont to do just after waking, the thought gained momentum as the minutes ticked by, his sleep addled brain providing outlandish yet compelling justifications for the bold act. 'Cimarron is south of here,' he thought 'Maybe Rucker passed by the ranch on his way to wherever he's going next.' He could imagine Alouicious arriving at the ranch just in time to rescue the McCall family from a flood, thwarting the nefarious schemes of neighboring sheep ranchers, and training a rattlesnake to guard the villains until the U.S. marshal showed up, all before breakfast. Peabody chuckled at the absurdity his sleepy brain had produced, but the niggling thought of traveling to the McCall ranch stubbornly refused to subside.

The fact that Peabody had nothing else to do was the final justification that caused him to give in to the notion of traveling to Cimarron, and he thrust the covers back from his bed energized at having a clear course of action. He performed his ablutions thoroughly, knowing that being able to wash was a luxury one could not expect when traveling through such sparsely settled lands as these, and neatly packed his valise, carefully organizing his notes and wrapping them in a piece of leather he kept to protect the paper from inclement weather. Shouldering his bag, he left his room neater than when he had arrived and headed down stairs.

While checking out of the hotel, Peabody inquired of the man behind the desk about local livery stables, and receiving directions, headed purposefully out the door. He had no trouble locating the livery in such a small town and soon he was negotiating with a horse trader, trying to find a mount whose price would match his meager funds.

"I'm afraid fifty dollars is more than I can afford" said Peabody, as he and the horse trader looked over what was available in the lot.

"Well, I'm sure we can work something out," mused the horse trader, who had introduced himself as George. The horse trader was a small rather greasy man who chewed a gargantuan lump of tobacco and wore shabby clothes which were seemed far too large for his slight frame. "You're from back east somewhere ain't ye?"

"Why yes, if you consider Memphis, Tennessee to be back east" replied Peabody, confused by the shift in conversation.

"Out here, most places are back east," said George "I guess I can let you have that little grey for thirty-five, and I've got an old saddle out back I'll let go for five more." George had worked as a teamster in St. Louis before the war and the hustle and bustle of the busy town's traffic had given him a deep and abiding hatred for all people who lived in large cities, and he considered any town big enough to have an intersection 'large.'

Peabody looked at the horse in question, it was small to be sure, with the slim, long legged look of many of the cowponies he had seen people riding since he got to town. The city bred reporter was no expert in horse flesh, he could ride of course, but he had never developed the discerning eye for the animals that men seemed to achieve after months or years of continuously working with the animals. To his unpracticed eye, the horse seemed all right to him, having all the qualities that a good horse should, namely four legs and a place to sit.

"Done," agreed Peabody, offering to shake "I think I'll call him Sunshine."

George shook the reporter's hand warmly, overjoyed to unload one of the most evil horses he had ever had the misfortune of owning on one of the hated townsmen.

Peabody's trepidation at the thought of riding all the way to Cimarron on his own was overcome by his desire to see Eunice again as soon as possible, so it was with little hesitation that he sent a dispatch by telegraph to his editor informing Mr. Johnson of his plans and purchased provisions he felt necessary for the journey. The shopkeeper at the general store directed Peabody to the trail that would take him to Cimarron, which was made conspicuous by the hooves of the cattle and horses which were regularly driven to the railhead. The saddle that the horse trader had sold him was old, but seemed to fit the pony well and the spacious saddle bags were sufficient to hold the prodigious amount of supplies and gear that Peabody had purchased at the general store as insurance against every contingency he could imagine.

It was almost noon before Peabody felt that he was sufficiently ready to be underway. Unhitching Sunshine from the rail in front of the general store, he grasped the saddle horn and swung himself into the saddle. Immediately the pony shied and sidestepped, the abrupt motion startling Peabody, who reflexively pulled on the reins and let out a quavering 'whoa horse' which caused the pony to rear, dumping his would-be rider unceremoniously into the dusty street. As Peabody rose and dusted himself off, he looked at the Sunshine, who stood calmly in place with what appeared to be a challenging look on his face. Peabody blinked and looked again, and the illusion disappeared, and the pony once again took on the appearance of a dumb animal to Peabody's eyes.

Unbeknownst to Peabody, the pony now known as Sunshine had been born wild in Texas, captured and semi-broken by a Comanche man, traded to a white man who taught the horse what a saddle was, if not its proper use, traded again to another white who put shoes on him, and yet another who had branded him. The pony had submitted to all of these indignities eventually, but he had never made any step of the various processes easy on any man, and he was not about to start now.

Not for him was the crude pitching, bucking and biting that his less intelligent brothers engaged in. Such artless tactics only brought retaliation, escalation of hostilities, and eventually a trip to the soap factory. No, the trick to dealing with men was to cause just enough aggravation so that one was never selected to perform much work, and when the opportunity for escape finally came, that none of them would search very hard to find and return one to slavery. Many men had used many adjectives in many languages to describe the pony, some fit for print, others less so, but none had ever used the word which so closely encapsulated Sunshine's mindset: cunning.

Peabody was unaware of any of this, as he clambered back into the saddle, this time with no trouble at all. Being used to city horses (which were useful enough brutes, though not usually very spirited) Peabody had no idea that the mind of a horse could contain any thought more complex than eat, sleep or pull. To Peabody, the idea that men still had to move about on living creatures was vaguely uncivilized, and the sooner that horses could be replaced by clean, sturdy machines, the better, but with no other options available to take him to his dear Eunice, Peabody tried to get comfortable in the saddle and gave the pony a little kick, which the horse responded to instantly, breaking into a brisk trot.

It took considerable effort to get Sunshine to settle into a smoother gait, as the trot jarred Peabody's spine mercilessly. If he hadn't known better, Peabody would have thought that the small horse was being purposefully difficult, jerking its head sharply against the reins before responding to any course correction and breaking into a bone jarring trot at every opportunity. But the pony proved to be an able mount, quickly covering miles with a strength that never seemed to flag. Peabody though, quickly grew tired, unused to so many hours in the saddle, and when he dismounted at a small creek to make camp for the night, his hips, and thighs were aching terribly. Making it to the ground with only a small groan, Peabody unsaddled and hobbled the horse the way the liveryman had showed him, but had no energy to set much of a camp, and simply rolled into his blankets at the base of a tree, quickly falling asleep despite the discomfort of the lumpy earth beneath him.

Having had little sleep the previous night, and being exhausted from only the half day of travel he had accomplished, Peabody slept soundly, not waking until the shooting pain of the cramps in his legs jolted him awake to find that the sun had already climbed well into the sky. His cries upon waking startled Sunshine, which was beginning to suspect he had jostled the man to death; as he had certainly tried hard enough.

Agonizingly gaining his feet, Peabody stumbled to the creek and drank deeply, making every attempt to stretch his cramping thighs and hips when he had slaked his thirst. Finally feeling like he could once again manage to walk, Peabody made his way back to his horse, and fed the beast some oats, taking only a piece of hardtack to break his fast, before replacing the saddle and removing the hobbles. His legs still felt too stiff to mount so Peabody decided to walk the first few miles, leading Sunshine across the creek and following the trail south.

"Come along Sunshine," he said patiently, after the pony had yanked his head back in an attempt to pull Peabody's arm out of socket "Eunice is waiting."

Sunshine wondered what a 'Eunice' was as they walked slowly down the trail. It must be something important, for they hadn't turned back yet, despite the horse's best efforts to wear the small man out. The gray pony began to feel a grudging respect for the man who led him, and revised his initial estimate of what it would take to be rid of the man who fancied himself Sunshine's master.

Days of mighty struggle later, Sunshine felt that

he was nearing victory. He had used every method he knew, and even invented a few more to make Peabody's trip as miserable as possible and as a result the pony was exhausted, but as he considered the shambles of a man which emerged painfully from under his blanket Sunshine knew it was only a matter of time before the man gave in and released him. The slight man had lost his hat when the horse had reared in the middle of a goodly sized creek, dumping the man into the bitter cold of the snowmelt, yet the man had held the reins the whole time and remounted without a word when the two reached the other side. When the sun rode high or a violent rainstorm came swooping down the prairie, Sunshine avoided any cover, causing Peabody to be alternately badly sunburned, and drenched with chill rain, but when the weather was pleasant Sunshine walked as close as possible to the juniper and cedar trees, assaulting his foe with every branch he could walk under. Thus Peabody was a wretched sight as he rolled his blanket and secured it behind his saddle, his hide was scratched and peeling, his hair was tangled with mud and grass and his formerly neat clothes were tattered rags.

Every morning of the miserable trip, Peabody had faithfully brushed Sunshine, feeding him oats and inspecting the pony's feet before mounting for the day's travel. He had always believed in taking good care of animals, in the same way one would take care of any valuable possession, but after the harrowing trip, the normally patient Peabody was sorely tempted to smash the wretched pony over the head with the biggest rock he could lift and take his chances on foot. Approaching Sunshine with the feedbag, Peabody paused, once again noticing the calculating look on the pony's face. Since leaving Las Animas, Peabody had begun to suspect that this particular horse was far more intelligent than he had ever believed possible, as the pony seemed to take pleasure in doing the very thing that would cause his rider the most pain and discomfort at any given time.

Peabody thought that his mind was definitely becoming addled by the arduous journey that the horrible pony had inflicted upon him, as ridiculous thoughts of a horse being cunning and malicious were very unlike him, but when he offered Sunshine the feedbag and the pony calmly stepped on Peabody's foot there was no mistaking the self-satisfied look on the horse's face.

Sunshine suspected that this would be his chance as he placed his hoof on Peabody's foot and leaned, putting just enough pressure on the man's toes to cause pain without disabling him. The horse knew that if he broke the man's foot, that Peabody would have no choice but to ride, but by leaving him ambulatory, Sunshine left open the possibility that his captor would finally be fed up and run the pony off in frustration. Sunshine expected Peabody to unleash a great cry of pain, possibly followed by an expletive, but the man simply grew very still, his only movement to drop the feedbag at his feet.

"Sunshine, have you ever heard of the Chiricahua people?" said Peabody grasping the bridle and turning the horse's head to gaze firmly into his eyes. "No? Why let me tell you about them. The Chiricahua Apache have eluded capture by the army for decades. How have they done this you ask? Well, they steal horses you see, and then they ride them as fast and as far as they can, without stopping for days, until the poor beast founders, then as the horse lays dying, too exhausted to struggle, they butcher the beast and eat him" explained Peabody in deadly calm tones "and if you don't get off my foot right now and behave yourself, we won't stop in Cimarron. We'll keep heading south until I find a desperate Chiricahua renegade and I'll sell you to him for a song. Then I'll laugh as he rides you away, knowing that you'll be on your way to the fate you deserve."

Of course Sunshine understood none of what the man had said, but no human had ever spoken to him in such a threatening manner. The horse had tried everything he could think of to break the man's will and just looking at the man, it was obvious that Peabody was exhausted, and in a great deal of discomfort, but the soft exterior that the man had displayed when the journey began had been stripped away, to reveal an iron will which Sunshine suspected he was no match for. Not wanting to make any sudden moves, lest the crazed man carry out whatever dire threat he had made, Sunshine slowly removed his hoof from Peabody's foot, whickering gently in submission.

Peabody calmly went about breaking camp, and mounted Sunshine without another word. Not until he was firmly seated and underway, did Peabody allow a single tear to march down the ravaged skin of his sunburned cheek, for he knew that if the horse saw him react to the agony in his foot, he would lose any advantage he had just gained.

The rest of the journey went much more smoothly for both parties once Peabody and Sunshine had reached an understanding. Peabody began to recover from his harrowing ordeal now that he didn't have to fight his mount every step of the way, and Sunshine, who had always looked upon the human race with nothing but contempt, found that his respect for the tough little man was becoming genuine affection as the miles rolled by. Compared to the hardship he had suffered during the first part of the journey, Peabody found the remainder of the journey easy going, discovering a peace in the wilderness he had never experienced in the city.

Soon they reached the village of Cimarron in the New Mexico Territory, and even though Peabody had come to enjoy the solitude, he was relieved to finally reach his destination where he hoped to find fresh clothes, a bath and a bed. The rough journey had left his valise battered but intact, and his notes had survived with just a little dampness encroaching on the edges. The rest of his belongings however, had not been so lucky, along with losing his hat in the creek, his coat and pants were filthy tatters, and the normally fastidious Peabody would not have been seen dead in them if there had been any other choice. Thus despite his ravenous hunger, and debilitating fatigue, he visited the general store first, purchasing a new pair of breeches, a homespun shirt, tall boots and a wide brimmed hat to provide some relief from the sun. Peabody felt foolish as he looked at his reflection in the window of the general store seeing a sun burned cowpoke staring back at him, but Cimarron was not cosmopolitan enough to support a tailor, so he had little choice in what garments he purchased. Instructing the shopkeeper to burn his old outfit, which was beyond salvation, he asked for and received directions to the livery stable and the barber.

Peabody led Sunshine to the livery first, feeling that the little horse deserved a rest and some pampering after their long journey. As he passed Sunshine's reins to the man who ran the stable, he warned the man to be careful since the little horse could be intemperate at times, but the man condescendingly told Peabody not to worry as he was quite good with horses. The liveryman led Sunshine away, and Peabody smiled as he heard a cry of pain and a muffled curse from the inside of the stable as the little horse taught the self-proclaimed horse wrangler a lesson.

Peabody had taken many baths in his life, but none had ever felt as good as the one he lowered himself into at the barber shop. The hot water felt nice, but Peabody did not waste time luxuriating in the heat before he began to scrub himself clean of the layer of filth that had been accumulating on him since he left Las Animas. When he climbed out of the tub at last, he finally understood what was meant by the phrase 'cleanliness was next to godliness', since the feeling of finally being clean was truly a blessing. Sitting in the barber's chair, he accepted his first shave in a week and as the barber scraped the heavy stubble from his chin he slowly began to feel human again.

After getting cleaned up, he made his way to the hotel, eagerly anticipating a warm meal and a soft bed. He was well into his second bowl of stew when his thoughts turned to the real reason he was supposed to be in Cimarron, and he asked his waiter if he had ever heard of a man named Alouicious Rucker.

"The name sounds familiar," the waiter replied, dredging the waters of his memory "say, wasn't that the name of the man who taught his dog to play cards? We all got a kick out of that one when we heard it."

"So you do know the man?" asked Peabody, hoping the man would tell him that Rucker was nearby and not send him to some far away place in search of his quarry.

"I don't guess I know him," said the waiter "one of the boys brought in a newspaper from back east a few days ago and we read all about it."

Peabody was surprised at the relief he felt when the man did not know the whereabouts of Rucker, for if he had no leads about where to search out the man he could justify spending some time here, and hopefully call on Eunice.

"Are you familiar with the McCall ranch?" he asked.

"Of course Mister, that's a pretty big outfit in these parts" the waiter replied "the big house is only a day's ride west of here. If you're hoping to hire on it's a good time, I hear a bunch of their boys are bringing in five hundred head from down south any day now."

Peabody thanked the waiter for the information, and finished his stew. Despite his weariness he wanted to jump up and head for the McCall ranch immediately, but he knew that both he and Sunshine could use the rest, and so he checked himself into the hotel, and made his way into his room, collapsing on the bed and falling sound asleep.

Even though he had gone to bed quite early, Peabody slept through the night, not waking until after dawn the next morning. He awoke refreshed as if the soft hotel bed had drawn the fatigue from his body like a poultice. Peabody poured the basin full of water and washed his face, he didn't need to dress, as he had fallen asleep fully clothed, and he grabbed his valise as he headed down stairs.

After a hearty breakfast and several cups of coffee the reporter made his way to the land office, hoping to find a map of the region surrounding Cimarron in order to plan his next move in his search for Rucker. Peabody knew he was distracted by the idea of seeing Eunice again, but he wished to remain diligent in his pursuit of Rucker, not only out of fidelity to his employer, but to further research the book he planned to write, which judging by the extent to which the news of the man had traveled, was sure to be a hit. Finding a huge map of the northern half of the territory on the wall, Peabody studied the area, there were several small villages scattered over the vast region, but all the roads seemed to connect in one way or the other to Santa Fe. Surely anyone who was traveling through the territory or at least news of them would eventually reach what amounted to the hub of northern New Mexico. And as luck would have it, the road to Santa Fe would take him to the west, where Eunice's uncle had his ranch. It appeared that he would not have to deviate from his duty to see Eunice after all. Excited, Peabody left the land office and headed straight for the livery stable to retrieve Sunshine.

Sunshine appeared to have had a restful night

as Peabody led him out of the stables. The stable hand had refused to fetch the horse, demanding his fee and insisting that Peabody remove Sunshine from the premises at once. Peabody was not sure exactly how Sunshine had overstayed his welcome, but he bet the pronounced limp that the liveryman exhibited had much to do with it.

Saddling Sunshine, Peabody checked his gear, or what was left of it. He had lost most of the odds and ends he had packed in Las Animas during the arduous trip south, but worried little as he would never have had use for most of it anyway. He stopped briefly at the general store, and picked up a box of Lucifer matches and a rain slicker, but except for a little provender, he saw little need to replace most of the items he had thought so necessary only a week ago. Sunshine seemed pleased to be so lightly loaded, and the two put the morning sun to their backs and headed west toward Santa Fe by way of the McCall ranch.

A pleasant day's journey found Peabody and Sunshine approaching the big house of the McCall ranch. Smoke rose from the chimney and several people were in evidence going about their mid morning chores. Peabody halted a polite distance from the house and hailed the folks, causing a pause in the activity and the nearest person, a towheaded boy of about ten to approach.

"My name is Peabody Samuelson, from

Memphis, Tennessee;" Peabody said "is this the McCall ranch?"

"Yessir," replied the boy, "I'm Jake McCall and this here ranch belongs to my Pa"

"Is Mr. McCall about then?" asked Peabody "I'd like to have a word with him if I could."

"He's yonder fixing the doctoring pens," Jake said indicating the pens which could be seen in the distance "we have five hundred head coming in soon and they need to be ready to go"

Peabody missed what the boy said next, as Eunice stepped out the front door of the house and onto the porch, raising her hand to shade her eyes against the sun. To Peabody, she seemed the very vision of beauty as she looked toward him. For a moment, Peabody was let down at Eunice's lack of reaction to his arrival, but it occurred to him that with his new clothes she probably didn't recognize him as he was still a good distance from the house. Not wanting to get off on the wrong foot with her uncle by speaking to her without permission, Peabody simply tipped his hat to Eunice, excused himself to the boy, and turned Sunshine toward the stock pens that Jack had indicated, resisting the impulse to urge the pony into a sprint.

Arriving at the stock pens, Peabody found two men working to replace a split rail; he recognized Buster, the man tasked with chaperoning Eunice during her journey west, and the other he assumed was her uncle.

"Hello," Peabody called as the men halted their labors to watch him approach.

"Howdy" said Mr. McCall guardedly, "What can we do for you?"

Climbing down from his horse, Peabody offered his hand to the rancher, "My name is Peabody Samuelson of Memphis; I met Buster and your niece on the train and wondered if I might have a word with you."

Recognizing Peabody as he drew closer, Buster closed his eyes and let out a breath, he had dutifully told his employer about the potential suitor they had met on the train, but had hoped to never see the man again, as McCall was less than pleased at Buster's failure to protect his niece from the advances of a stranger.

"I've heard of you," said McCall giving Buster a dark look "What can I help you with?"

"I admit I'm embarrassed to be so forthright Mr. McCall," said Peabody, his already sunburned face reddening further, "but Eunice and I got along well during the train ride, and I was hoping to be allowed to call on her in the future."

"We'll have to see about that," replied McCall

noncommittally "How about you give us a hand fixing these pens and we'll talk it over."

Peabody had little experience with manual labor, but what he lacked in skill, he made up for with hustle as the men set about the work. Mr. McCall was doubtful to begin with, but over the course of the day, he warmed to the earnest polite little man, and when the dinner bell rang that evening, he invited Peabody to stable Sunshine in the barn and join them for dinner.

After he had made sure that Sunshine was comfortably settled in the barn, Peabody cleaned himself up the best he could and made his way to the house. His heart seemed to flutter in his chest at the thought of having dinner with Eunice and her family, and his hands shook as he knocked on the front door. He was greeted by Buster who ushered him into the dining room where most of the family was just taking their seats around a large table. Just as he was pulling back his chair, Eunice entered the room carrying a large steaming pot.

"Eunice, I believe you know Mr. Samuelson" said Mr. McCall uncomfortably.

"Hello Eunice, it's nice to see you again," said Peabody winning the prize for the understatement of the decade.

Eunice stopped dead in her tracks still holding the large pot of beans. She had been told that there would be company for supper, but neither her uncle nor Buster had told her that it would be the man she had pined for since her arrival at the ranch.

"Why Mr. Samuelson, what a pleasant surprise," said Eunice, recovering from her shock and placing the pot on the table.

Throughout dinner the two young people only had eyes for each other, as they both picked at their food, making polite small talk with the rest of the family. Afterward, the whole family retired to the porch to enjoy the cool night air, and the conversation meandered hither and thither with talk of many things, none of which Peabody or Eunice would later remember. When the night grew late, Mr. McCall retired, bidding Peabody to bunk in the barn and with the unspoken signal the rest of the family went inside as well.

Lying awake in the hayloft, Peabody could not remember ever having a more pleasant evening, and he found himself wishing that this life could last forever.

The following days proved to be as enjoyable as the first, as Peabody spent his days working around the ranch with Mr. McCall and Buster, and eating his meals in the pleasant company of Eunice and her family. His lack of experience with ranch work was a liability that was more than compensated for by Peabody's enthusiasm and willingness to learn. Sunshine became ever more loyal to Peabody as the days went by, but the other people of the household quickly learned to give the recalcitrant horse a wide berth.

The men were hard at work digging a shallow trench which would funnel the water which fell from the eaves of the house to the garden area rather than into the nearby arroyo, when young Jack spied a rider cresting a ridge to the south. As the rider drew near, Buster was the first to recognize one of the ranch hands which had been sent to drive the newly purchased herd back from Lincoln. Greeting the cowboy warmly, Mr. McCall asked how the trip had gone as the herd was arriving later than he had expected.

"It was rough but we made it," the cowboy answered "the herd should be coming over the ridge within the hour."

"What kind of trouble did you have?" asked Buster.

"Those longhorns were wild as deer when we picked them up" said the cowboy "we played hob keeping them headed the right direction for the first little while, and they stampeded pretty bad down round Santa Fe."

"Anybody hurt?" asked Buster.

"None of ours, but a few boys who were carrying the mail were in the wrong place at the wrong time. One of them died and another was in pretty bad shape when we left him with the doctor in Santa Fe" lamented the cowboy.

"Dern, that's bad luck," said Buster.

"Did you get their names?" asked McCall "Maybe we can send their families something."

"The mail carrier was Old Bob Blackwood, and the other old boy was a drifter by the name of Alouicious Rucker, I never was clear on which one passed away, I stayed with the herd while some of the other boys went to get help in town" explained he cowboy.

The group was startled at the clatter of the shovel falling from Peabody's suddenly nerveless fingers.

Chapter 12

*Any attempt to understand the legendary Alouicious
Rucker without first understanding his friends and
enemies is destined to fail. For a man is defined by the
company he keeps, and he is judged by the strength of
his adversaries.*

*--excerpt from "Al Rucker: a Western Legend" by
Peabody Samuelson*

Leading the outlaws across the dusty plain
without getting murdered was even more difficult than
Kessay had thought it would be. Riding southwest from
the North Fork of the Canadian, Kessay had led the men
across the parched land into Texas, crossing the
northern tributaries of the Canadian River with just
enough regularity to keep them from dying of thirst.
Both the men and horses were beginning to suffer from
the arduous journey across the sun baked plains.

Kessay kept the men on a course far enough
north that the Canadian River itself was never in sight,
for if the whites discovered that they could simply
follow the river west all the way into the mountains of

the New Mexico Territory their need for a guide would be at an end along with his life. Kessay did not fear Abel and Jean-Batiste, as they both seemed to be pleasant, even gentlemanly at times, but the leader of the outlaws, Logan, was a vicious man whose disregard for life of any kind went far beyond pragmatism.

Kessay sometimes pitied Abel and Le'Chiffre as the Indian was sure that if not for Logan, the other men would have long since given up the chase for this 'Rucker' fellow, and moved off to more hospitable climes. Logan's quest for vengeance however would not be denied, and it was clear that the meeting between Logan and his adversary would result in the death of one or the other. Though he had never met the man, Kessay found himself rooting for Rucker in the confrontation which was coming as sure as day followed night.

Kessay set a relentless pace for the band, figuring that if the horses and men were exhausted when he made his move and left the outlaws, his chances of escaping the desperado's clutches would be greatly increased. The Indian never doubted for a minute that the vengeful Logan would chase him when he ran off, and if the outlaw ever found out that a much easier trail across El Llano was available, Kessay would quickly find himself on Logan's list of people which needed killing. As they headed deeper into the New Mexico territory, Kessay knew they were headed into higher country, and once the outlaws reached a point where they could be confident of finding water for themselves, he would be as good as dead. Watering their horses at a small creek, Kessay decided it was time to set the stage for his departure from the company of desperados.

"From here it is a long way to the next water" he said affecting his best 'noble savage' voice "We should rest here for the night and press hard in the morning."

"Looks to me like we're getting into better country, higher anyway," said Logan.

"No," replied Kessay, pointing across the creek "It drops back down beyond that ridge in the distance and after that its fifty or sixty miles of sand dunes."

"I don't see a ridge" said Abel, squinting in the direction Kessay indicated.

"It must be farther than a white man can see" said Kessay sagely.

Logan glowered at the Indian suspiciously as Jean-Batiste covered his mouth and turned away, having difficulty keeping a straight face at the audacity of the lie. During the long journey Le'Chiffre had often suspected that Kessay was not leading them on quite the best route through the plains, but the Cajun had kept his mouth shut, knowing that challenging the Indian's truthfulness would only lead to a fight which would end with Logan killing the Apache, and leaving them in this desolate place without a guide of any kind, which was as good as a death sentence. Besides, Jean-Batiste had come to like the funny little fellow who adeptly played to Logan's preconceived notions about Indians, masterfully weaving a skein of prevarication in such a way that even the con man often couldn't discern the truth. Le'Chiffre couldn't be sure what Kessay's game was, but as the bleak reality of their situation left them at the Indian's mercy, he would let it play out, gambling that they wouldn't be scalped before it was all over.

"Where does this creek end up?" asked Abel, gesturing to the south.

"It empties into a shallow brackish lake," responded Kessay, not meeting the man's eye "No fish, no grass, a poison wasteland as far as the eye can see."

With that pronouncement Le'Chiffre knew exactly which direction they should head if the Indian escaped from under Logan's watchful eye and they found themselves without a guide: south to where there was something that Kessay did not want the outlaws to find.

Abel Beckwith was tired. Tired of the wind, tired of the heat, tired of the thirst, and most of all, tired of his brother. Ever since that day at Logan's hideout, Abel's life had seemed to be one long, drawn out ride, through boring, empty country, sleeping on the ground or not at all, subsisting on hardtack and jerky. Abel craved the comforts of a town as he had never craved anything before. He dreamed of gambling halls, saloons and hotel mattresses. Abel enjoyed Jean-Batiste's company, and was even amused by the weird proclamations of the Indian, but his brother's maniacal determination to run Rucker to the ground had become wearisome many days ago. From what Logan had told Abel, it was by sheer accident that the man had run afoul of the outlaw outside Memphis, and the hillbilly could hardly be blamed for the actions of his dog on the river barge, so Logan's unjustified vendetta which would have been humorous in other circumstances, made Abel worry for his brother's sanity in this desolate wasteland.

Abel could tell by the look on Logan's face that he planned to murder Kessay as soon as they no longer needed him, which they would probably get away with, as killing an Indian was barely a misdemeanor in the territories, but if Logan gunned down the hayseed, they would probably be on the run for the rest of their lives, a prospect which was unattractive to say the least. Thus Abel found himself wishing to come across a town, where he and Le'Chiffre could take their leave of his brother, making a living 'mining the miners' and not be drawn into the life of a desperate outlaw.

That night, after the sun had set, the four men sat around a small campfire which was set a little way back from the creek. The wind had picked up, bringing with it the distinctive smell of moisture so rarely sensed in the arid plains. Kessay knew he was out of time, for if morning still found him in the company of the desperados, they would quickly discover his ruse about the land they were headed to, and his chances of surviving his ordeal would drop from slim to none.

Detecting the sound of fat raindrops hissing as they fell into the smoldering buffalo chip fire, Kessay settled back on to his haunches, chewing the piece of hardtack he had been offered, hoping and praying that the rains would come heavy and give him the cover he needed to escape Logan's clutches during the night.

"Looks like it could be a wet one tonight," said Abel, glancing up as a raindrop stuck the brim of his hat. "I could use a bath, but this ain't what I had in mind."

"I dreamed about having a nice hot bath and a shave last night," lamented Jean-Batiste "I'm afraid this traveling through the wilderness does not agree with me, I was made for feather beds, hot meals and maybe a glass of wine shared with a sporting woman, not deprivation such as this."

"You girls wear me out with your complaining," groused Logan "do you forget why we're out here? That son of a buck Rucker is out there laughing at us, spending the reward money he got for ruining our lives, while we follow this troglodyte across hell's front lawn.

We can't let that stand."

Abel and Jean-Batiste rolled their eyes at one another at the renewal of the wearisome tirade which they had been subjected to almost continually since leaving St. Louis.

"We've got to be in the New Mexico territory by now, I hear there's good gambling towns in New Mexico, maybe we should stop when we find one and rest a spell" suggested Abel, not wanting to feed Logan's ire by commenting on Rucker.

"Santa Fe can't be far, and this time of year there are plenty of cowboys passing through ready to spend their hard earned wages on a friendly game of cards, we could make a lot of money if we work together" agreed Le'Chiffre.

"We'll stop in town just long enough to ask around about Rucker, but we ain't out here to play no cards" said Logan darkly.

Fed up with Logan's stubbornness, Abel stood his ground "Logan, we're almost out of money and food, at this rate, even if we find that turnip merchant, we'll be ragged and half dead from starvation, I say we find a town, stay awhile and get our bearings. Heck, we don't know the country that well anyway, how do you expect to find one man out here?"

"We'll find him no matter how long it takes, find

him and kill him" said Logan quietly.

"You'll get us all scalped or hung more likely, and killing that kid won't bring Flora back" argued Le'Chiffre, his irritation with Logan flaring as he stood up to face the madman.

Lightning flashed just at that moment, the light glinting off the barrel of Logan's pistol which was suddenly aimed at Le'Chiffre's face. Jean-Batiste was shocked, having never even seen the man move, as one second Logan had been standing by the fire with his arms crossed, and the next he had his revolver leveled with every appearance of someone who meant to use it. Jean-Batiste knew he had pushed the volatile Logan too far and closed his eyes preparing himself for oblivion. The sharp click of a cocking pistol rang loud, even over the sound of the now steadily falling rain, but rather than the report of the gun, the next sound Jean-Batiste heard was Abel's voice:

"Put it down Logan, you don't want to do this."

Cracking open one eye, Le'Chiffre was shocked to see Abel was standing as well, with his pistol aimed at his own brother.

"Stay out of this Abel, this doesn't concern you" said Logan uneasily.

Abel let the ridiculous statement pass, keeping his voice and his hand steady "Just put it away and let's get some rest Logan."

"Rest hell, I won't tolerate any more lip from this Cajun son of a bitch" said Logan, his eyes betraying doubt about his dire course of action.

Despite his hesitation, Logan would have surely carried out his threat if Jean-Batiste had not at that moment said quietly: "The Indian is gone."

The shock of the simple statement broke the stillness of the deadly tableau, as Abel and Logan turned to look about the camp, quickly confirming the absence of their guide.

"Come on boys, we got to catch him," said Logan, holstering his pistol and moving toward where they had the horses picketed.

"We'll never find him in this," Abel said, gesturing to indicate the rain slicing through the darkness "Let's just get some rest if we can, and head out in the morning."

"He took one of the horses, he'll be miles away by morning" argued Logan.

"He's gone, let it go, big brother" said Abel calmly.

Relenting, Logan brought the remaining horses closer to camp and tied lead lines to their saddles which they used as pillows. The three exhausted men spent an uncomfortable night in the rain, waking regularly fearing the wily Indian would return for the rest of their mounts.

Kessay rode slowly once he crossed the creek to conserve his horse's strength which was flagging quickly after the long journey across El Llano. He hoped the rain would wash away the horse's tracks, but true to the capricious nature of weather on the high plains, the storm lasted only long enough to wet the ground before abating. As the transient clouds parted revealing the quarter moon, Kessay looked back and was discouraged to see the obvious trail that his horse had left through the sticky mud which could be followed by a child. Not the best of luck, but maybe he wouldn't be followed anyway. While he was sneaking away from the camp, the desperados had been ready to kill one another, and if Logan had been shot then the odds of the others following him on their own were slim. Hoping this was the case but not willing to rely on the slim chance that Abel had killed his own brother, Kessay reluctantly urged his mount into a trot and headed due south, making for the Canadian river.

Kessay reached the Canadian just after daybreak, the slow muddy river the most blessed thing he had ever laid eyes on. As he dismounted, he noticed his horse was trembling with exhaustion; he had made it to the river in the nick of time, as he figured that once the sun came up that Logan would be hot on his heels, and his horse was not up for a chase. Letting his horse water, Kessay looked up and down the river, wondering which would be the best direction to take in order to avoid the outlaws. Doubling back to the east might throw off his pursuers, but he doubted they would be fooled by such an elementary trick, at the same time, the men were traveling west and if he went that direction, he was sure to cross paths with them eventually. One choice seeming as good as the other, Kessay led his horse upstream to the west hoping to find a spot where he could hide while the outlaws passed by.

The three men broke camp in silence before dawn, none wanting to mention the tense situation of the previous night. As the men crossed the creek and guided their mounts west, the silence was broken by Logan who gruffly ordered Abel and Jean-Batiste to spread out and search for the Indian's trail. The two men obeyed without a word, both more than willing to be alone rather than suffer the tense discomfort of Logan's presence.

Abel found the tracks bearing southwest a short time later, and gave serious consideration to riding on without telling the others in order to spare the beleaguered Indian Logan's ire, but not knowing which direction would lead them to water, Abel felt he had no choice, and signaled his companions by firing his pistol into the air. Soon the outlaws once again rode together in grim silence following the tracks as they turned south, until they reached the Canadian River.

"That Indian said there was nothing but a brackish lake this way," said Abel, finally breaking the silence which had prevailed for most of the morning.

"We probably could have followed this river all the way into New Mexico," said Le'Chiffre, silently applauding the cunning little Apache.

"If I'd have known that, I would have shot him as soon as we saw him" said Logan.

Abel and Jean-Batiste looked at each other, guessing that was probably the reason that Kessay had declined to mention it.

"The tracks lead into the river, he probably doubled back to the east" said Logan as they moved forward to water the horses.

"Unless he thought you would think that, in which case he went west" replied Abel glancing at Jean-Batiste and cracking a smile for the first time in days.

"Or if he thought you though that he would think that, then he went to the east," continued Jean-Batiste, taking his cue from Abel.

"What are you two rambling about?" asked a confused Logan.

"It's the classic poker player's conundrum," replied Le'Chiffre warming to the topic "Can you determine how many levels ahead your opponent is thinking and think one more level beyond that?"

"And at what point do you end up thinking in circles and choose a course of action at random?" continued Abel "Usually the one who gives up first ends up penniless at the rail."

"But in this case we have a slight advantage," reasoned Jean-Batiste "The river runs west to east, and we want to go west, therefore we can simply ignore the Indian and follow this river until we reach a settlement."

"What do you say Logan?" asked a hopeful Abel, "Let's just get out of here."

"All right, west it is," said Logan relenting in the face of the con man's logic "But if we ever come across that Indian again I'll make him wish he had never been born."

Traveling upriver was much easier on both man and horse than crossing the plains had been. Abel and Jean-Batiste's mood improved greatly as they made steady progress west, but Logan felt a deep sting to his pride in knowing that he had been played for a fool by an ignorant savage. This humiliation had not been public as the blow Rucker had dealt to his pride had been, but that didn't mean it stung any less. Logan's murderous thoughts, which had long been consumed by visions of only Alouicious Rucker, soon expanded to include Kessay, who he silently vowed would not escape his retribution for long.

It was by pure chance that Le'Chiffre discovered where Kessay had left the river that afternoon. Heeding a call of nature, the Cajun's modesty prompted him to take advantage of the steep banks of an arroyo which ran into the south side of the river. Gazing at the ground in the idle contemplation which comes upon a man at times like these, he was surprised to find himself looking at what was clearly a portion of a lone horse track. Finishing his business and investigating further, he found that the Indian had apparently left the river and traveled south following the arroyo bottom, brushing his tracks away for a goodly distance and with such skill that the Indian's path would never have been seen if Jean-Batiste had not decided to stop where he did. Le'Chiffre gazed at the tracks for just a moment before tipping his hat in the direction they ran and returned to join his companions. He felt light hearted as they rode, knowing that the cunning little man had evaded Logan's clutches, at least for now.

It took another day of hard riding before the outlaws reached civilization. If you could even call it that, Abel thought, considering the small fort they had discovered at the confluence of two rivers. Compared to the seemingly endless expanse of short grass prairie they had just passed through however, the outpost was a metropolis.

Approaching the fort, the outlaws were a little

concerned about being recognized, despite the fact that none of them had been in this part of the country before, and any pursuit from St. Louis or Memphis surely had not reached this far into the territories. Even if the authorities of the lonely fort were on the lookout for them, with their provisions depleted and being totally lost, the three men had little choice but to approach the garrison and seek food and directions, so after coming to an agreement on what false names to use while at the fort, the three desperados rode into plain sight of the encampment and hailed the sentry on picket duty.

"Howdy," called the soldier in response to Abel's greeting "Where you boys headed?"

"Well, we ain't rightly sure about that," said Abel, giving the soldier a sheepish smile and affecting his best imitation of a countrified rube "We was on our way back from taking a herd up to Fort Dodge and got a little turned around, which fort is this?"

"This is Fort Bascom in the New Mexico Territory," replied the soldier, "You cowboys ought to stick to the mail route if you're going to get lost in the territories." with the false sense of superiority that only a man at the bottom of the figurative totem pole can muster.

"An Indian made off with one of our horses and we've been chasing him for two days," interjected

Logan, glowering at the haughty soldier, "I thought it was your job to keep the savages on the reservation where they belong."

Jean-Batiste inwardly winced at Logan's caustic remark, and seeing any chance that the army might aid them quickly vanishing in the expression of the soldier, he doffed his hat and quickly adopted an apologetic air.

"Please forgive my friend," Le'Chiffre said, indicating Logan, "for the pony the Indian took was his favorite, being his only companion for many a long mile on the trail."

"Because nobody else could stand to be around him is my guess," the soldier responded, giving Logan a challenging look.

Seeing the wisdom in Le'Chiffre's play, Logan choked back a bitter retort, knowing that to antagonize the soldier would only increase their difficulties. But beneath the affected veneer of submission, Logan added the young soldier to the list of people he planned to get even with as soon as possible.

"Well you-all had better come up to the fort, the Captain will want to hear your story" said the soldier.

"Much obliged sir," said Abel sticking with the humble cowboy routine, "our horses are plumb tired out and we ain't had a hot meal for quite a spell."

After seeing to the needs of their horses, the three outlaws masquerading as cowboys were introduced to Captain Charles Avery who was the commanding officer of Fort Bascom. The captain had a shock of white hair and massive mutton chop sideburns which looked rather ridiculous, but to underestimate Charles Avery would be a mistake. Captain Avery was a driven man, who took his duty seriously, engaging in aggressive campaigns to root the Kiowa and Comanche out of the Llano Estacado which met with limited success. Therefore when he heard the story of a renegade Indian stealing a horse in what he considered his backyard, Captain Avery wasted no time in ordering a squad to pursue the thief and bring him to justice.

The U.S. Army graciously supplied the three cowboys who had reported the theft with a loan of fresh horses so that they might accompany the squad and positively identify the culprit. So it was that after a hot meal, and a good night's sleep, the three outlaws sallied forth from Fort Bascom to track down the renegade Kessay, accompanied by five heavily armed soldiers.

Kessay had set an easy pace for both himself and his horse after making sure that the desperados had passed him by, he eased along, mostly on foot, letting the jaded steed rest as much as possible and all the while thinking that the outlaws had long since lost his trail and given up the pursuit. Therefore it was with some surprise that as he rested at the base of a low juniper near the top of a ridge he saw eight riders crest the ridge to the east following his exact trail down the slope. He had been watching his back trail, not out of genuine concern that he was being followed, but out of long habit, handed down by his father before him, for people who relied on raiding for much of their income quickly learned to keep a close eye on their back trail or quickly became dead.

Kessay was not curious enough about the approaching riders to wait around to find out who they were, and he eased himself out from his resting place and moved with slow deliberation to retrieve his mount, which was tethered nearby. Taking care to keep the low trees between him and the riders so as not to silhouette himself against the sky, Kessay led the horse over the ridge and mounted, turning due south and quickly riding away at a right angle to his original direction of travel, making for a rocky butte less than a half mile away.

Reaching the bluff he guided his mount behind an oblong boulder which had fallen from the butte at some point in the distant past, and turned to look back, as the group of riders crested the ridge he had been sitting at not long before. Exactly as he had feared, the riders paused for only a moment at the spot where he had turned south before turning their mounts to follow the clear trail he had intentionally left. There was no doubt now that he was being pursued, and considering that only the three outlaws had any idea he was in the area, there was little doubt in Kessay's mind about the identity of his pursuers. Logan Beckwith was after him.

Kessay's antecedents had been evading the U.S. army for generations, avoiding pitched battles, raiding at various places and melting into the landscape, but that didn't make it easy. The dogged pursuit continued for two days, the Indian leading the soldiers on a circuitous chase, through creek beds, over rocky promontories and down treacherous grades, using every trick he had ever learned to lose his pursuers, but the whites stubbornly persisted, and it was all Kessay could manage to stay one step ahead of the soldiers.

Now the chase was over, his horse was played out and would go no farther, he had no more tricks up his sleeve, and the mounted soldiers were only a few miles behind him. Kessay unbridled his horse and left it near a small stream striking out on foot up a rocky slope where he hoped to find a spot to make his last stand. The Indian was not an idealistic hero like some of the men who had defied the army for so long, but he held no illusions about Logan Beckwith's intentions and when the two met, Kessay was determined not to go out without a fight.

The ancient rattlesnake rested in the hollow under a rock which he had claimed as his own, and wondered if it was worth the effort of moving into the sunlight to try to get warm. Lately it had become more and more difficult to maintain a temperature that didn't make him feel uncomfortable. The chill of the shade caused the snake's old bones to ache and the heat of the warm rocks gave him a headache. The rattler had seen more winters than any other snake he knew, and during last winter's den time all the other snakes had seemed like mere children to him, giving him the patronizing false respect that all creatures in their prime give their elders.

Small wonder (the snake thought) as his eyes and heat sensitive pits had become weak through the passage of years, his scales had become ragged and dull, his once thick, proud rattle had been torn off in a battle with a vicious roadrunner and even his venom had lost its potency, being barely strong enough to stun the mice which strayed too close to his resting place.

Mired in self-pity, the venerable serpent considered that he would rather stay where he was and let the cold take him when the den time came than make the long trek to the nearest den only to face another summer of trying to choke down struggling ground squirrels. Shifting his aching bones, he moved out of the shade and settled into a comfortable place on the hot flat rock which he hoped would ease the pain in his joints at least for a while.

No sooner had he reached the familiar spot though, than a shadow passed over him, robbing him of the comforting rays of the sun. Dreading a cloud, which might herald a rainstorm, the old snake looked up and through his clouded eyes he could barely make out one of the tall beasts which went on two legs like a bird, crouching down in front of him. Reflexively his tail began to vibrate back and forth, making him lament once more the loss of his once proud rattle. The tall beasts called men were often dangerous, but the bitter old rattler was in no mood to yield one of his few remaining resting places and decided to make a stand (figuratively of course, for snakes do many things but standing is never one of them). Hoping his withered old glands could at least produce enough venom to make the man uncomfortable for a while; the ancient snake launched himself forward and felt the satisfying sensation of his fangs penetrating meat.

Kessay located a place of concealment near an outcropping of rocks, where he could not be encircled and drew his small knife and tested the edge with his thumb. He found a position with a good field of view and tried to decide on an avenue of attack which would give him the best chance to get in at least one good lick before he was gunned down. He chose what he thought was his best bet and imagined driving his knife into Logan's vitals as he crouched beside a boulder to wait.

No sooner had he settled onto his haunches than a pain like lightning shot through his calf, causing him to quickly spring back to his feet. Turning to seek the source of his agony, Kessay was horrified to see a massive rattlesnake coiled behind him ready to strike again. The Apache were not overly superstitious, but snakes were one of the exceptions. Not just rattlesnakes but snakes of any kind, were considered bad luck and were not to be touched, looked at or even crossed paths with. If a right thinking Apache spotted a snake's trail in the dust, he would drag his feet across it so as not to step over the path of the loathsome creature. Thus the sight of the massive, ugly rattlesnake which had just bit him was too much for the exhausted Kessay to cope with and he fainted dead away.

Abel Beckwith's hopes of finding rest and comfort upon reaching civilization had been dashed by Logan's insistence that they accompany the squad of soldiers sent out after the Indian. A mere one night's sleep in an army bunk and one hot meal had done little to help him recover from the deprivations that they had endured crossing the Indian Territory before they had set out once again hot on the trail of someone he had no desire to catch.

It was clear that Kessay knew he was being followed as the men tracked the Indian through the rolling hills and rugged mountains of the New Mexico territory. Backtracking repeatedly, losing the trail and finding it again, the outlaws were disoriented by the dizzying route they took through unfamiliar territory, but the soldiers knew what they were about and being better mounted, the party had narrowed the gap and felt they were drawing near to their quarry.

Shortly after noon on the third day of the

pursuit, one of the soldiers spotted the missing horse standing near a small creek which ran along the bottom of a steep canyon. Fearing an ambush, the soldiers scouted the area and approached the horse cautiously, finding the steed to be quite jaded but in otherwise good health.

"If that Indian took off on foot, we'll never find him in this mess," said the sergeant in charge, indicating the rugged country around them "I think it might be time to head back to the fort."

"And just let the Indian get away?" asked an outraged Logan.

"If you can track an Apache through the cliffs, be my guest" replied the soldier "after you find him come and see us, we'll have a job waiting for you."

The other men of the squad snickered as they mounted and prepared to head back to Fort Bascom.

"You can head back with us and gather up your horses, they should be rested by now, from the fort you can make it to Santa Fe easy enough" said the sergeant eager to be rid of the unpleasant Logan.

"A few days in Santa Fe sounds like just what we need," said Abel "what do you say, Logan?"

"I agree with Abel" said Jean-Batiste "a few days of good food, a roof over our heads and the company of a senorita would not go amiss."

Frustrated by Kessay's escape, but not knowing what else to do, Logan relented, and the outlaws moved to follow the soldiers out of the canyon and back toward Fort Bascom, none noticing the unconscious man lying on the ridge only a few hundred yards away.

Chapter 13

It may seem to you dear reader, that Alouicious Rucker was a solitary man, with only his steed and hound for company. While this was sometimes true, Rucker also gained many allies in his quest to bring peace and righteousness to the lawless west, befriending people of many backgrounds and stations as he traveled the territories.

--excerpt from "Al Rucker: a Western Legend"
by Peabody Samuelson

Ruck awoke at the sound of someone pulling aside the curtain which acted as a door to his room and turned to look at the woman who entered bearing a steaming bowl on a tray. She was a plump but handsome woman, some years older than Ruck, with wavy black hair which showed isolated strands of gray and brown expressive eyes framed my lines which indicated frequent laughter. She wore a flowing red skirt and modest white bodice which suited her nicely.

"*Buenas Dias,* Senor Rucker, how are we feeling today?" asked the woman placing the tray on a small table near the bed and turning to straighten the blanket covering Ruck.

"Much better Mrs. Chavez, thank you" replied Ruck, eagerly sitting up in bed, anticipating breakfast. It was true; for the headache which had incapacitated Ruck for the three days since he had regained consciousness had faded to a dull ache which he suspected would pass soon enough once he got some fresh air. He remembered little of the stampede which had left him unconscious, but the doctor's family which had kindly taken him in had filled him in on what details they knew as he recovered.

Ruck had been found senseless on the ground by the cowboys whose herd had run him to the ground, and the men had taken him into Santa Fe. Dr. Chavez had treated him in his office until he regained consciousness and then taken him into his home where he would most benefit from Mrs. Chavez's exemplary nursing skills. Ruck was sore and bruised all over, but had mercifully suffered no broken bones, his worst injury being the blow to the back of his head which had left him senseless for the better part of a day, and sleepy and nauseous for another three.

As for his companions on his journey from Las Animas to Santa Fe, Josiah had escaped the stampede unscathed but Old Bob had been found dead on the banks of the arroyo having sustained terrible injuries from the accident. Ruck had wanted to go to the funeral, but when he had tried to get out of bed he became dizzy, falling heavily back with his vision darkening and nausea washing over him. Seeing his condition, but unable to speak English, the doctor had told his wife who interpreted for him, to forbid Ruck from going to the funeral of his dear friend. Too sick to argue, Ruck had fallen back into a deep sleep and when he had awoken, Old Bob was in the ground and Josiah was once again on his way back to Las Animas, knowing his beloved uncle would want the mail to continue without him.

Doctor Lorenzo Chavez and his wife Leticia had nursed Ruck back to health, feeding him spicy but tasty meals, and kindly seeing to his every need. Their son Aureliano had visited Ruck many times, keeping him company and teaching him some Spanish. Ruck was amazed, and more than a little touched when little Aureliano had related the story of the stampede as told by the cowboys who had brought him in.

Apparently after he had fallen, Bolliver and Whitey had stayed by his side, protecting him from the maddened cows which streamed around them. Whitey had been slightly injured, but Aureliano's father had showed him how to tend the dog's minor wounds and soon Whitey was on the mend, limping around the yard, but never straying far from the house where Ruck lay.

"What's for breakfast this morning?" asked Ruck eagerly. Mrs. Chavez was a wonderful cook, and

Ruck had grown fond of the spicy, exotic dishes that she had so far presented.

"*Menudo* I just made this morning" replied Mrs. Chavez, smiling as she placed the tray with the steaming bowl over Ruck's lap "It's a kind of soup with *tripas* flavored with *chile*, it will make you strong."

"It smells delicious," said Ruck gratefully before digging in. The dish delivered what the smell had promised as the soup was wonderful, the texture of the tripe was unusual but not unpleasant, and soon Ruck had finished his first helping and quickly overcame his embarrassment enough to ask for another.

"I'm glad to see that you are hungry again, Mr. Rucker," said Mrs. Chavez bringing him his second bowl, "Dr. Chavez says you should be able to get out of bed today if you are feeling up to it."

"I think I could manage it," said Ruck, manfully chewing to subdue the rubbery tripe "I would like to check on Bolliver and Whitey, Aureliano said they saved my life."

"The cowboys could speak of little else," agreed Mrs. Chavez removing the tray and the empty bowl "Aureliano has been taking good care of the animals, but I think they would be glad to see you. It seems strange but somehow the mule especially seems very worried about you."

"That's Bolliver all right," said Ruck smiling "he always did seem to think more than any honest mule should."

"I will bring your clothes, so you can get dressed and see your dear friends the mule and the ugly dog" said Mrs. Chavez with a teasing smile.

"*Muchas Gracias*" replied Ruck.

When Ruck emerged from the adobe house Whitey was there to greet him, burying his nose into Ruck's shirt sleeve and snuffling heavily as if he had missed his dear friend's scent. Ruck's eyes grew misty as he scratched Whitey behind the ears, having underestimated how much he had come to love the weird looking cur. Their reunion was interrupted by a sharp familiar braying, and Ruck looked up to see Bolliver standing at the rail of a nearby corral with ears pointed forward looking nothing less than relieved to see his old friend on his feet again.

Whitey turned and ran toward Bolliver as Ruck rose and headed toward the mule at a slower pace. The mule too seemed to exult in Ruck's particular scent, taking in great draughts of air in his nostrils and blowing noisily when Ruck approached. Tears threatened to breach the levees of his eyelashes as he stroked Bolliver's neck, murmuring assurances of his well-being to the clearly concerned mule.

"I have taken good care of them, Senor" said

Aureliano, having seen Ruck emerge from the house and come running after abandoning his chores.

"I can see that," said Ruck kindly "I'm much obliged to you for that, Aureliano."

"Will you be leaving soon, now that you are all better?" asked the boy.

"If your father says I'm all right to travel, I reckon I will," replied Ruck.

"Where will you go?"

"I set out for the Arizona Territory; I guess that's still where I'm headed" Ruck said, thinking about his journey so far and eagerly anticipating the road ahead.

"You should not go there Senor Ruck," said Aureliano "the Apache live there and they will get you."

"I don't guess I have much that an Indian would want," chuckled an amused Ruck.

"My friend Carlos says they will cut off your hair and set you on fire!" continued the precocious boy.

"Then I'll just have to wear my hat," said Ruck, teasing the boy.

"Wait here, I just remembered something," said Aureliano sprinting back toward the house and emerging shortly with Ruck's hat.

"The cowboys brought it when they left you here, I mended it and found a feather for it" said the boy handing Ruck his old hat. There was a new tear which had been carefully stitched, and a large owl feather, banded white and grey was stuck in the band protruding at an angle toward the back of the hat.

"It looks as good as new, "said Ruck, touched at the gesture "Thank you, my friend."

After another day of convalescence, Dr. Chavez declared Ruck fit to travel and it was with no small regret that he collected his things and saddled Bolliver, making ready to continue his journey alone. Mrs. Chavez had echoed Aureliano's warnings of the Apache when he spoke of his ultimate destination, but Ruck would not be swayed, stubbornly holding to the goal he had set for himself when leaving Tennessee. The Chavez family was reluctant to accept money from Ruck, but he insisted as it was the least he could do for the family who had saved his life and nursed him back to health. It was an emotional but silent farewell as none trusted their voices to remain steady through a long good-bye, and only little Aureliano was humble enough to gently cry as Ruck rode away.

Despite a persistent headache, Ruck felt heartened to be back on the trail once again. His brush with death beneath the thundering hooves of a stampede had not improved his opinion of cows much, and so he gave the main trail running south from Santa

Fe a wide berth to avoid the many herds of cattle which were surely being driven north to the railheads this time of year.

The empty rolling grasslands which had so shocked him when he had first seen them from the train, had begun to grow on Ruck, and he settled into the tranquility of the lonely vistas as if he had been born to them. Ruck was in no hurry to get anywhere, and Whitey still walked with a slight limp, so he set an easy pace, often dismounting to lead Bolliver through the land which changed little over many miles.

Bolliver and Whitey seemed to have developed a greater understanding and respect for one another after their shared trial in and around Santa Fe. Standing shoulder to shoulder to protect their friend Ruck, then waiting and worrying through the long days as he mended, had tempered Bolliver's dislike for the dog and eased Whitey's frantic efforts to gain the approval of the mule. When Whitey was nearby, he trotted steadily along beside Bolliver, close enough to enjoy the company, but no longer a constant nuisance. The few times that the dog strayed behind Bolliver, the mule let the dog pass without trying to kick the dog into oblivion making for a more peaceful journey than they ever had before.

Toward the end of their third day out of Santa Fe, Ruck pointed Bolliver toward a nearby canyon, seeking a place to camp for the night out of the wind which seemed to be ever present on the rolling plains. Drawing near the rim of the canyon, Ruck was delighted to see a small stream running along the bottom of the canyon and praised the Lord as he sought a path down the slope to the bottom of the defile. Finding a likely spot, Ruck dismounted and led Bolliver down the relatively shallow grade.

Picking their way around a pile of boulders Ruck was startled to see a body lying on the ground only a few yards away. Hurrying quickly to render what aid he could, Ruck slowed as he saw that the man was an Indian, who was coming to as if from a swoon. The Indian's eyes snapped fully open at Ruck's approach and both hesitated as they saw one another. The man on the ground was still for only an instant before raising a trembling hand and pointing toward the base of the rock next to which Ruck was standing.

"Snake," the Indian uttered in a quavering voice.

Turning where the man indicated, Ruck saw that there was indeed a huge rattlesnake poised to strike just a few feet away. Puzzled, he wondered why he could not hear the buzz of the snake's rattle even though its tail was clearly vibrating. Shrugging at the mystery, Ruck drew and cocked his pistol with one smooth motion, drawing a bead on the serpent and tightening his finger on the trigger when the Indian stopped him:

"Don't shoot, there are bad men nearby," the Indian said in the odd tones of one trying to whisper loudly.

Casting a wary eye about without seeing anyone, Ruck took the man's word for it and eased the pistol's hammer down with his thumb.

"Can you walk? Let's get away from that thing" said Ruck, matching the Indian's whispering tones.

"I am bit, but I think I can walk" replied the man in a, halting accent which sounded strange to Ruck's ears.

Ruck helped the Indian to his feet and the two eased around the rock pile giving the snake a wide berth.

"Where are you bit?" asked Ruck, when the men had reached safety, drawing his handkerchief from his pocket and twisting it preparing to make a tourniquet.

"Here," said the Indian, indicating his calf "I fear the serpent has done for me."

"You're an optimistic fellow ain't you?" said Ruck as he located the two pinholes in the man's red-brown skin and tied the rag around the man's leg above them "What's your name?"

"I am Kessay, of the White Mountain Apache

tribe"

"Apache, huh?" said Ruck as he cleaned the blade of his pocket knife on his shirttail preparing to cut the wounds and draw the poison "I heard you boys were tough, I guess we're about to find out. Brace yourself Kessay."

Kessay ground his teeth as Ruck sliced deeply into his already aching calf, but didn't cry out fearing that Logan and his boys might come upon them at any moment. As the white man lowered his head to suck the poison from the wounds, Kessay noticed that the man wore an owl feather in his hat, and the sight made him groan in fear. Like snakes, owls had supernatural significance to the Apache as harbingers of death. Kessay had never before put much stock in such things, but after being bit by the cursed serpent and then ministered to by a mysterious stranger who proudly displayed the feather of a messenger of doom, his shock addled brain was suddenly willing to believe.

"I guess that's all I know to do" said Ruck, after drawing several mouthfuls of blood from the wounds "Let's go find us a place to camp that has fewer rattlers."

"Who are you?" asked Kessay.

"Alouicious Rucker, lately of Tennessee, pleased to make your acquaintance," replied Ruck offering his hand to help Kessay to his feet.

"Rucker," breathed Kessay, stunned at the revelation that this was the man Logan Beckwith sought so intently "I know some men who are looking for you" he said simply.

Seating Kessay on Bolliver, the men moved up the canyon and located a concealed place to camp without seeing the outlaws whom Kessay insisted were in the area. They set no fire and the night air became brisk with the onset of night.

Ruck was surprised that the men he had crossed paths with east of the Mississippi had joined forces and followed him halfway across the country, but Kessay's description of the outlaws matched what Ruck remembered of the men leaving no doubt as to the identity of his pursuers.

Kessay's snake bite was not nearly as painful as he had thought it would be which gave him hope, however slim, of survival. As they sat in camp lost in their own thoughts, the Indian silently vowed that if he lived, he would help the man who had come to his aid escape the outlaws who pursued him, or barring that, fight to the death by Ruck's side in any confrontation with Logan Beckwith.

Both men's minds raced with the revelations and events of the day as they lay in silence gazing at the thick spangle of stars spread above them until sleep finally came, leaving only Whitey to keep watch through the night.

Kessay was delighted when he woke to find that his leg though stiff, was not swollen or discolored as he had expected. Grateful, he silently renewed his vow that he would help Ruck, who he felt greatly indebted to.

"Where are you headed, Ruck?" asked Kessay as they broke camp.

"I set out for the silver fields of Arizona," replied Ruck, "I figure to head for Tucson then make a new plan from there."

"You're a prospector?" asked Kessay, puzzled at the lack of mining equipment.

"Not yet, but I thought I would try my hand at it. I hear there's plenty of silver for the one lucky enough to find it and I thought I might see the country, maybe find a good place to settle that ain't covered up with people" said Ruck, tightening the cinch on Bolliver's saddle.

"Tucson is too hot and dusty, you should come to my home, it's much better" offered Kessay.

"This whole country is hot and dusty from what I've seen," Ruck chuckled.

"This is paradise compared to Tucson," said Kessay, smiling and gesturing to the short grass plains around them "but our mountains are much better, and they are on the way to where you want to go. I will take you there and you can decide for yourself."

"Much obliged Kessay, I'll take you up on that" said Ruck, warming to the Apache man who was so different from the dire stories describing the tribe as sullen hard eyed savages.

Ruck offered to let Kessay ride Bolliver, worried about the Indian's injured leg, but Kessay declined, and the men headed west on foot, the shadows cast by the morning sun pointing the way toward the Apache homeland.

The two men traveled slowly, Kessay showing Ruck many tricks to avoid being spotted by their pursuers as they walked along. The men conversed about many things as the morning wore on, and finally Kessay worked up the nerve to ask about something that had been wondering about since the day before.

"You sure were quick with that pistol back there" Kessay mentioned matter-of-factly.

Ruck shrugged noncommittally "Maybe I guess, I don't like rattlesnakes much, so I just drew without thinking about it."

"A man who doesn't even carry a shovel, saying he is a prospector heading to the boom towns, one might think you were a gunfighter" said Kessay cautiously.

Rucker laughed, "No, I ain't a gunfighter, I guess I've shot plenty of game but never fired a gun in anger in my life."

Kessay relented but was unconvinced, as he remembered the smooth ease with which Ruck had brought his pistol to bear on the coiled viper. Kessay knew some men who reacted to stress by freezing up, but others he had seen, had cool instinctive reflexes and he suspected that Ruck was one of the latter. Either that or Ruck was a seasoned pistol fighter, but nothing in his manner had suggested to Kessay that he was anything other than what he seemed to be: a young man with the typical if slightly exaggerated wander-lust.

"Tell me about where you live," said Ruck, uncomfortable with the topic and eager to change the subject.

Kessay's eyes lit up with the mention of his homeland. "It's the best place I know of," he said "We live on the banks of the White River, where it runs through a steep canyon, there are pine and juniper trees all around, and pink and orange bluffs overlook the river where the biggest elk in the world come to drink from clear pools where golden fish swim. In the winter, a little snow falls, but usually melts quickly, and in the summer you can go up the hill where antelope run through grass as high as your knee."

Kessay's tone grew wistful as he continued: "In the springtime we would go to the river and make masks for the first dance of the year, and in the fall my mother would make the best acorn stew you ever had."

"Do the white folks give you any trouble?" Ruck asked knowing of the conflicts which had been ongoing between white and red men for generations.

"There is a little fort nearby, but we get along with them all right, and there's a couple of ranches to the north sometimes we trade with them, but so far we haven't had trouble like they have to the south" Kessay chuckled "Heck, some of us have even scouted for the army when the boys from San Carlos go renegade!"

Laughing at his new friend's mirth more than any understanding of the situation, Ruck was intrigued by Kessay's description of the place they were going, and looked forward to seeing the place for himself.

Chapter 14

Our readers will be saddened to note the grave injury of Alouicious Rucker who met with an accident while working with a herd of cattle. Rucker, for those who haven't followed the regular reports from our reporter in the field, is the man who captured the nefarious outlaw Logan Beckwith here in Memphis some time ago. We here at the Appeal wish Mr. Rucker a speedy recovery and will provide details of his condition when they become available.

--excerpt from The Memphis Daily Appeal
March 30, 1875

Eunice had wept softly as Peabody vowed to return to the McCall ranch with all haste after interviewing Rucker. Upon hearing the news of Rucker's accident, Peabody had quickly gathered all the information he could from the rest of the cowboys, and immediately set out for Cimarron where he stayed only long enough to telegraph the news to his editor back in Memphis. Remounting Sunshine he set a brisk pace toward Santa Fe.

Now, two days into the journey, his mind was still roiling with conflicting emotions. The story he had pieced together from the cowboys was as incredible as any he had heard about Rucker so far. Not for any heroism on Rucker's part, for by the time the cowboys had seen him he was already unconscious on the ground, but the way the cowboys had described Rucker's dog and mule defending their fallen master had dumbfounded the reporter. The fact that Rucker rode a mule at all came as a surprise to Peabody, as the vision the reporter had of Rucker as a heroic figure didn't fit with the idea of the man riding a humble mule. Nevertheless Peabody was fascinated by the story the cowboys had told, having never heard of such bravery in the animal kingdom before.

No sooner had Peabody heard that Rucker was laying in a sickbed in Santa Fe than the thought that he would have to be separated from Eunice hit him like a body blow. There was no doubt in Peabody's mind that he had come to love the bookish young woman and he lamented having to leave her behind even though his long sought after goal of meeting Rucker seemed to finally be within his grasp.

During the evenings after supper, Peabody and Eunice had sat at the table compiling the notes of his journey so far, working on the novel which Eunice was sure would be a hit. Eunice had faith in the man she loved, so when the news about Rucker had arrived, she had encouraged Peabody to pursue the lead, supporting him despite the heartache it caused.

Peabody had even come to enjoy the company of Mr. McCall and the taciturn Buster, as the camaraderie produced by sharing in hard work had taken deep root among the men. So it was with a curious mixture of eagerness and reluctance that Peabody had saddled Sunshine and rode away from the ranch promising to return as soon as the interview with Rucker was complete.

Upon entering Santa Fe, Peabody inquired about the whereabouts of the doctor from the first person he saw. Receiving directions, the reporter urged Sunshine into a lope through the dusty streets not wanting to miss his opportunity to complete the task he had set out for.

He found the office of Dr. Chavez easily enough, as the town was of no great size or complexity compared to Memphis where he had grown up. Quickly hitching Sunshine to the rail out front Peabody entered the door of the office which was open to the fresh spring air, to find the room occupied only by a lone Mexican man seated behind a desk.

"Hola, que puedo servirle?" the middle aged man asked, looking up from the notebook he had been writing in.

"My name is Peabody Samuelson," he said doffing his hat, hoping the doctor spoke English "I'm looking for Alouicious Rucker; I heard you were treating him."

"Buscas Senor Rucker? Por Favor venga conmigo" the doctor said in rapid fire Spanish as he stood and made for the door.

Peabody closed his eyes and let out a slow breath, fighting the urge to curse the skies. He didn't understand a word of Spanish and had no idea if the man he was addressing understood what he wanted or even if this was the doctor.

Luckily Dr. Chavez did understand what Peabody wanted and since the man was unarmed and clearly didn't understand a word of what the good doctor was saying, Dr. Chavez decided to take Peabody back to his house in the hopes that his wife could discover the intentions of the man who was seeking Ruck, who had become a dear friend of the family.

When Peabody's frustration had subsided enough that he felt he could open his mouth without uttering blasphemy, he opened his eyes to find the Mexican man putting on his narrow brimmed hat and gesturing toward the door. His hope that the man had understood him or at least was willing to take him to someone who did, was rekindled as he followed the man out the door and down the street, pausing only to unhitch Sunshine and lead him along behind as the men walked.

It was a mercifully short walk as the men strode along stewing in the discomfort that exists between people who don't share a language, and soon the men arrived in front of a white adobe house with the ubiquitous bunches of dried red chile hanging from the porch.

The Mexican man hailed the house and a pleasant looking Mexican woman emerged, drying her hands on a white towel. The man unleashed a staccato burst of Spanish which contained the word 'Alouicious' and the woman smiled warmly, coming down from the porch and extending a hand toward Peabody.

"Hello sir, my name is Leticia Chavez, and this is my husband Dr. Lorenzo Chavez, he tells me you are looking for Alouicious Rucker" said Mrs. Chavez in crisp English.

"Peabody Samuelson ma'am, pleased to make your acquaintance" said Peabody, doffing his hat, relieved that he had found someone he could communicate with "I'm a reporter for the Memphis Daily appeal, I'm trying to find Mr. Rucker for an interview, and I heard your husband treated him."

"You are a reporter from Memphis?" asked Mrs. Chavez doubtfully, looking Peabody up and down and taking in the half wild pony that he led.

Confused at Mrs. Chavez's obvious incredulity, Peabody looked himself up and down as well, and for the first time in what seemed like weeks considered what he must look like. The broad brimmed hat he held in his hands was sweat-stained from working on the ranch, and his homespun shirt and pants were dull and dusty from the trail. The big city reporter chuckled at the changes only a short trip through the west had wrought.

"I suppose I don't look like it anymore," said Peabody with some embarrassment, "but it's been a hard trip, and my good suit didn't survive it. I took the train from St. Louis to Las Animas Colorado and from there rode horseback all the way here by way of Cimarron. I've come halfway across the country just to interview Alouicious Rucker and I would be deeply indebted to the one who could tell me where he is."

Touched by the depth of emotion on Peabody's face as he described his journey, Leticia could see that the man meant no harm to her friend Ruck and made a decision on the spot.

"Come inside Senor, it is almost lunch time, I will tell you what you want to know" she said turning toward the house.

During the meal, the Chavez family came to believe that Peabody really was a big city reporter despite his common appearance as he eloquently regaled them with tales of his journey westward. The family in turn gave Peabody all the information he requested as he produced his notebook after Aureliano had cleared away the dishes.

Peabody was crestfallen to find that he had missed Rucker again, who had left six days earlier, this time for the silver fields of the Arizona Territory. Finding one man riding a mule in such a vast area would be like finding a needle in a haystack, and Peabody had to admit that this time he had lost Rucker's trail for good.

Far from being disappointed, Peabody was guiltily relieved that he had no way to chase Rucker any farther, and sitting at the Chavez's dinner table he made the monumental decision to wire Mr. Johnson his resignation and go back to the ranch, hopefully to marry Eunice.

He had never been more convinced of the rightness of a decision in his life, and the clarity of purpose let him relax and enjoy the afternoon, chatting with Leticia and Lorenzo while Aureliano played outside.

The spell of the pleasant visit was broken a little while later as Aureliano rushed into the house and excitedly declaring:

"Mama, there's another man here asking about Ruck!"

Looking out the window, Peabody's breath caught in his throat at the sight of Logan Beckwith walking toward the house.

Logan had grown sullen after they had left the trail of the Indian, following the squad back to Fort Bascom. Rucker and the Indian seemed destined escape his vengeance, as both had seemingly escaped into the vast wilds of the territories. Reaching the fort and retrieving the horses which they had stolen back in Missouri, the three had struck out immediately for Santa Fe, as Logan had no further reason to dispute Abel and Jean-Batiste's desire to spend time in town.

As they drew closer to Santa Fe, Logan became more withdrawn by the hour hardly saying a word as they rode, but Abel and Le'Chiffre had grew cheerful at the idea that their arduous journey through the plains seemed to be finally coming to an end.

Hundreds of monotonous miles through the plains had given Abel and Jean-Batiste many hours in which to develop plans and schemes which they would undertake once civilization was reached. The two con men were excited to try out their collaborations and parlay what little money they had left into a fortune in the cow towns and mining camps through fraud, graft and all manner of chicanery.

Entering the dusty pueblo early in the afternoon, Logan allowed himself to be led through town by his companions who made a beeline for the nearest saloon. Hitching their horses at the rail, the three made their way inside where Abel and Jean-Batiste were delighted to find a card game already in progress. The game was shorthanded and the two wolves had no trouble securing an invitation to lie with the lambs as Logan approached the bar and ordered a drink.

The two con men engaged in the friendly banter at the table, both playing a clumsy and unimaginative game, biding their time before making their move. The chatter around the table was typical, the two newcomers being pressed for news and receiving news in return.

"Where are you boys from?" asked the shabbily dressed mule skinner to Abel's left.

"We just came from driving a little herd up to Fort Dodge, decided to stop and play some cards on our way back to Lincoln" replied Abel amiably using his best hick impression.

"Did you cut across no man's land on the way here? That's pretty wild country" commented a buckskin clad trapper across the table.

"It sure is," replied Abel "one of our horses was stole by a renegade out there, but we made it out with our scalps still attached."

"Have there been many herds pass through lately?" asked Le'Chiffre, wanting to steer the conversation away from the thin fabrication the men were using as a cover.

"Oh a fair amount I suppose" replied the muleskinner "awhile back a herd of longhorns just off their winter range stampeded just outside of town, killed Old Bob the mail carrier and hurt another fellow pretty bad."

"That's a heck of a dose," said Abel noncommittally.

"He's all right now though, spent a few days over at Doc Chavez's place getting healed up and rode off a few days ago" said the mule skinner "fellow had a real funny name as I recall, what was it again Bill?"

"Alouicious Rucker, I believe" replied the trapper.

Abel's poker face barely held as he studied his hand, hoping against hope that Logan was not eavesdropping on the conversation. If his brother had heard the name it was only a matter of time before the three were off on another wild goose chase through the Indian infested hinterlands. His hopes were dashed however, as he saw Logan leave the bar and approach the table out of the corner of his eye.

"What did you say his name was?" said Logan menacingly.

"Alouicious Rucker" said the mule skinner nervously.

Laying his cards on the table, the normally loquacious Le'Chiffre for once encapsulated the moment with only one whispered word:

"Damn."

A revitalized Logan quickly obtained directions to the doctor's house and set out once again with his two reluctant companions in tow. He followed the directions with a singleness of purpose that he had lacked since losing the Indian, and soon the outlaws arrived in front of the doctor's house. A Mexican boy playing in the dusty yard paused at their approach and hailed them politely:

"Good morning, are you looking for the doctor?" asked Aureliano.

"Not exactly," replied Logan "We're friends of Alouicious Rucker, we heard he was here recently and would like to know where he went."

"Senor Rucker left a week ago, but you're in luck," said the boy enthusiastically "One of his other friends just arrived this morning, maybe you can find him together."

"Maybe so," said Logan as he dismounted from his horse.

"I will go tell him you are here," said Aureliano racing for the house.

Abel and Jean-Batiste looked at each other, silently wondering who this friend of Rucker's could be, and more than a little worried about what the volatile Logan would do to the friend of his enemy. Their fears were well founded as rather than wait for an invitation, Logan strode purposefully toward the door, his hand resting on the butt of his pistol.

As Logan reached the doorway, he did not hesitate but immediately drew and cocked his pistol, covering the three people in the room. A middle aged Mexican couple sat at the table in the front room across from a white man who looked like one of the cowboys who populated the region.

"I'm looking for Rucker, and if you don't tell me where he went, something very bad is going to happen to someone too young to deserve it." Logan pronounced simply as he pointed his pistol at Aureliano who was clinging tightly to his mother.

"We don't know where he went, that's what we were just talking about" said Peabody in a quavering voice.

"Maybe you didn't hear me," said Logan calmly, drawing a bead on the boy "If you don't tell me which direction he went the boy dies."

"Southwest, heading for the Arizona Territory" said Peabody submitting to the outlaw's ultimatum.

Satisfied, Logan relaxed his focus and turned toward Peabody, "You look familiar cowboy, have we met somewhere before?"

"I saw you in the Memphis calaboose Logan," said Peabody "I was interviewing Marshal Calloway about your capture."

"Dang, you sure have changed," said Logan taking in Peabody's simple dress and sun browned skin, "What are you doing way out here?"

Peabody made no reply as he silently prayed the outlaw would leave without spilling blood.

"I'll tell you what, if you see him before I do you can give him a message for me" said Logan.

"What message would you have me deliver?" said Peabody in an effort to placate the madman.

"Tell him I have a bullet for him too" Logan said before turning his pistol toward Peabody and pulling the trigger.

Hearing the gunshot from inside the house, Abel and Jean-Batiste knew their short stint as gamblers in Santa Fe was over and neither said a word as Logan emerged from the house and casually mounted his horse.

"Let's get out of here" said Logan.

"Where to now?" asked Abel.

"The Arizona Territory" said Logan simply as he spurred his horse into a gallop.

"Wonderful, I've always wanted to be tied to a wagon wheel and set on fire by savages" Le'Chiffre quipped as he goaded his mount to follow.

Abel did not comment, thinking that his life would be much easier as soon as someone killed his deranged brother.

As soon as Peabody hit the floor, Lorenzo rushed to his side, tearing open the wounded man's shirt to inspect the injury. Seeing that the bullet had entered Peabody's chest at a shallow angle, lodging in the shoulder, the doctor sent Aureliano to retrieve the traveling kit he took on house calls and struggled to stem the tide of blood flowing from the wound. Aureliano was quick, and came back with the kit as Leticia banked up the fire and set water on to boil, anticipating her husband's needs.

The doctor was forced to make an incision in the shoulder close to where he thought the bullet was lodged and after some careful probing with forceps, withdrew the lump of lead and cast it to the floor. Lorenzo quickly set about staunching the flow of blood, and was relieved to find the shot had missed the major arteries. The doctor soon had Peabody stable though still unconscious from shock and he sent Aureliano to the neighbor's house to get help in retrieving the stretcher he kept at this office.

Soon after the shooting, the competent Dr. Chavez had Peabody resting in his office having had applied the boiled poultice that Leticia had prepared and administered laudanum for the pain which would be severe when Peabody awoke. Having done all he could for the man, Lorenzo emerged from his office, to speak with the sheriff who had been waiting patiently to take a statement.

Peabody awoke the next morning groggy and unsure of where he was. As he moved to pull back the blanket he was covered with, pain shot through his chest and shoulder causing him to gasp, but gritting his teeth he pulled the blanket aside to inspect his injuries. His chest and shoulder were swathed in bandages showing a small splotch of blood and his left arm was bound across his stomach to prevent movement of the appendage. The pain focused his thoughts and brought back the memories of being shot by Logan Beckwith. Thinking he was lucky to be alive, Peabody settled back onto the pillow and closed his eyes, falling into a deep dreamless sleep.

A week later a much improved Peabody used his one good arm to clumsily sit up in bed, eagerly anticipating the meal which Leticia was bringing into the room. Peabody had spent his convalescence in the same bed where Ruck had recovered from his injuries after the stampede, and the thought was humorous to Peabody as the frustration of trying to catch up with the man had long gone past the point where it could be borne with anything less than laughter.

Dr. Chavez's tender ministrations and Leticia's patient nursing had seen Peabody through a slight fever and carried him far along the road to recovery, his left arm was still tender, but he could move it now without reopening his wounds and Lorenzo's prognosis was optimistic.

"Thank you, Mrs. Chavez" said Peabody as Leticia placed the tray over his lap.

"*De nada,* Senor Samuelson" replied Leticia, carefully pronouncing his name.

"This smells wonderful" he said, tearing off a slice of tortilla and using it to scoop a bite of chicken into his mouth.

"Thank you," said Leticia, "I have some bad news, Peabody"

Given pause by her uncharacteristic use of his first name, Peabody looked up at Leticia, noting her uncomfortable demeanor as she fidgeted at the side of the bed.

"What news is that?" inquired Peabody patiently, at a loss as to what could affect the stalwart

Mrs. Chavez so.

"The posse who went after Logan Beckwith returned today," she said, looking down at the floor "what was left of them anyway."

"What do you mean?"

"Of the eight men who went out only five returned, the sheriff was not among them." Leticia said quietly.

Stunned, Peabody put down the tortilla, his appetite having flown, "Did the deputies who came back say what happened?"

"*Si,* the posse was ambushed in a canyon, the sheriff and two others were shot from their horses. The rest of the posse fired back but were unable to capture any of the outlaws. The posse returned here to get help from the marshals or the army. The Sheriff was a friend of ours" she said, tears welling up in her eyes.

"I'm sorry for your loss" he said gently. Peabody was surprised at the revelation, for in all the years Logan Beckwith had been on the run from the law in Tennessee, he had never ambushed a posse. The man was known for his ability to evade pursuit with preternatural ease, but to turn at bay and engage in a gunfight with the law seemed out of character for the outlaw. Logan had to know that the killing of a lawman would only increase his notoriety resulting in an expansion of the manhunt already in progress. It seemed to Peabody that the already bold outlaw was becoming more reckless as he drifted farther west and the thought made him fear for the safety of anyone who found themselves a target for Beckwith, namely Alouicious Rucker.

"Have the marshals started out after them yet?" asked Peabody.

"Word has been sent to Amarillo and El Paso, and it is expected that the marshals will begin their search in a week or so" said Leticia, clearly worried at the implications.

"In a week Logan will have killed Alouicious and disappeared" said Peabody with the certainty of one familiar with the depredations the outlaw had committed around Memphis. Seeing the despair clearly written on Leticia's face, and feeling a loathing for Logan Beckwith that he had never felt before, Peabody came to a conclusion which would have been quite unlike him only a few weeks before.

"I have to find Rucker before Logan does" said Peabody, "get him to the safety of a city or fort, if only to give the marshals a chance to muster."

"It is too soon for you to travel Peabody, and you don't even know Alouicious, why would you risk you life to save him?"

"It's not for him that I have to do this Mrs. Chavez, it's for you, and for Aureliano, and for everyone else who is in danger as long as that madman is on the loose" said Peabody, his conviction growing with every word "If Logan kills Rucker, he will disappear, and we would never know who will be next" he said as Eunice's face rose to the surface of his thoughts.

Leticia relented, running to fetch Peabody's clothes as he rose from bed and tenderly removed his arm from the sling. His head swam as he stood for the first time in a week, but his strong conviction kept him stubbornly standing, and saw him through as he dressed and made his way out the door where Aureliano waited with Sunshine, Mrs. Chavez having sent the boy to fetch the horse.

"You had better get a different horse, Peabody" said Aureliano rubbing his shoulder "this one tried to pull my arm off twice on the way here."

"Yeah, he'll do that," replied Peabody simply as he gingerly mounted the pony "Where is the general store? I'll have to get supplies."

"Down there and turn left on Main Street," replied Aureliano.

"Be careful, Senor Samuelson" called Leticia, as Peabody turned Sunshine down the street.

Peabody only nodded, gritting his teeth against

the pain in his shoulder.

Fearing a long journey, Peabody purchased plenty of food and water, getting the shopkeeper's help to load his supplies into Sunshine's saddle bags. On the way out the door, something propped against the wall caught Peabody's attention and on impulse he asked the shopkeeper:

"How much for the shotgun?"

Chapter 15

In retrospect, it seems not at all surprising that a man with such charisma and indomitable will as Rucker could survive among the deadly Apache, but when the stories of a white man living among the savages first began to emerge from the terra incognita of the dreaded Apacheria, belief was beggared in all God fearing people who heard it.

--excerpt from 'In Pursuit of a Legend, a Memoir' by Peabody Samuelson

The land where Kessay's people dwelled was all he had described and more. On foot, leading Bolliver, it had taken the pair many days to traverse the vast grasslands of the western New Mexico territory, the ubiquitous spring winds proving to be the only truly bad weather the men encountered while crossing the flat terrain. The two had kept a sharp lookout for other travelers, wary of crossing paths with cavalry soldiers or the Beckwith Gang but despite Whitey's far ranging scouting expeditions they saw no one as they passed through the empty landscape of western New Mexico.

As the elevation increased, the grasslands gave way first to low cedar and juniper trees, then to taller pines and aspens as the men entered the Arizona territory. With the passing of the days Whitey's limp had slowly disappeared, Ruck's headaches had dissipated, and Kessay seemed to suffer no ill effects from his snakebite, thus it was a healthy, high spirited bunch that crested the pass through the White Mountains and began the steep decent into the canyon where the White River ran and Kessay's people made their home.

The treacherous footing at the head of the canyon contrasted sharply with the flat prairies which had dominated their trip through the New Mexico Territory. As they picked their way down the rocky slopes, the aspen trees disappeared and the pines began to be interspersed once again with junipers and even the occasional high country cactus. Soon Ruck could make out the sound of swiftly moving water over the susurrus of the wind in the trees. Cresting a hogback Kessay paused, and pointed to the floor of the canyon not far below.

"Whiteriver," Kessay said simply in a wistful tone uncharacteristic of the normally taciturn Indian.

Despite the beauty of the landscape, Ruck was nervous about entering an environment which was so alien to all he had ever known, and as the men approached the village Ruck wondered if he had made a mistake in accepting Kessay's invitation. The village was made up of numerous huts and ramadas, each fashioned from branches and grass and among them Ruck could make out many Indians going about their daily chores. Several dogs began barking at their approach and the nearby villagers turned from their tasks to investigate the commotion.

Kessay hailed the nearest person in a halting, sibilant language which sounded strange to Ruck's ear, and soon the two men were surrounded by a group of exited Apaches who all seemed to be trying to talk to Kessay at once. Ruck stood a little away from the group, not wanting to intrude on the homecoming, but almost immediately, Kessay was gesturing to Ruck and people began to approach him offering to shake hands and speaking to him in words which he could not begin to understand.

Just as Ruck was beginning to feel overwhelmed by the warm but indecipherable reception, the attention of the entire crowd was drawn to the sound of a high pitched voice calling Kessay's name. Looking toward the sound, Ruck saw a young woman sprinting toward them, and he was instantly struck by the girl's beauty. Her gleaming black hair streamed behind her and shapely legs flashed from beneath her skirt as she ran toward Kessay with outstretched arms. The woman's dark eyes and beautifully angular face shone with joy as she embraced Kessay, clutching him tightly in a joyful reunion. Ruck assumed that this was the sweetheart Kessay had mentioned, and thought his friend must be the luckiest man in the world as the two broke their embrace.

"Ruck, I want you to meet my sister Magashi," said Kessay.

Ruck was surprised at the revelation but recovered quickly, "Alouicious Rucker actually, pleased to make your acquaintance, ma'am," he said politely removing his hat.

"It's nice to meet you too, Alouicious Rucker," replied Magashi, pronouncing his name in the same halting accent her brother had, yet with melodious tones that struck Alouicious as the sweetest sound he had ever heard.

Whitey loved Whiteriver. New sights and smells greeted him around every corner in a seemingly endless world of new discovery. Numerous other dogs roamed the village forming small packs whose territories and allegiances changed hourly, resulting in a massive, endless war-game. Whitey was unfamiliar with the complex hierarchy the dogs of Whiteriver had organized, but after only a few short hours, the snarling and snapping which comprised the canine political process had run its course and Whitey had a tentative idea of his position relative to the others. Being the newcomer, Whitey was fairly low on the figurative totem pole, but by the end of the first day he was allowed to participate in some of the varied projects alongside the other dogs, chasing squirrels, begging for food, and peeing on various things being the main activities of the day.

Bolliver too found the area around the river much to his liking, as the deep canyon blocked most of the wind which had been relentless during the journey across the plains and succulent green grass grew deep along the riverbank. Ruck had unsaddled and combed the mule before leading him to the banks of the river where a few horses, cows and sheep grazed along the river, and Bolliver found himself hoping that their long journey was finally over as he enjoyed a well deserved rest. Whitey came to check on him a few times throughout the day, accompanied by a different group of dogs every time, and each time Bolliver gave his friend a reassuring whicker before returning to his repast, sending Whitey off to engage in whatever mindless pursuit the dogs had planned.

Ruck had difficulty keeping his eyes off Magashi, as the group settled into the shade of a ramada and ate a lunch consisting of a thick stew which Kessay informed him was made from acorns and mutton. The conversation was clearly light and cheerful, though Ruck could understand none of what was said save that which Kessay or Magashi translated for him.

"Where did you and Kessay learn to speak English?" Ruck asked Magashi as she settled down near him with her own bowl of stew.

"Our father had us learn from a man named Carter who lives up the hill," she replied gesturing to the north. "He thought it would be good for us to be able to speak with our neighbors."

"Are there many white people around here?" asked Ruck.

"Yes, there is an army camp down the canyon, and some others keep cows on big ranches at the top of the hill, and of course some are always around looking for gold or silver."

"Have they found any yet?" asked Ruck, fearing the idyllic canyon would be swarming with people if it had.

"We heard one of them found silver down by San Carlos a while back and already there is a town springing up across the big canyon, but none closer than that yet. Did you come here looking for silver?" Magashi asked casually, taking another bite of stew.

"Yes I did, I've never prospected before but things back home weren't going so good so I came west looking for a fresh start, I have had enough of Tennessee and I want to find a quiet place to settle that's not already covered up with people"

"You don't like people?" asked the woman

looking up at him from under her thick eyelashes.

For some reason he could not identify, the question made Ruck blush, "That's not it exactly, since I came west I've met a few people that I like very much" said Ruck looking into Magashi's eyes feigning courage he didn't feel.

Magashi smiled and looked away without responding. The look on her face emboldened him and despite his trepidation he plunged deeper into the maelstrom of his unfamiliar emotion.

"You have a pretty name, does it mean something?" he asked.

Magashi gave an embarrassed chuckle, "Yes, they call me Magashi Bi'jag which means 'cow legs' because my legs are so thick and lumpy."

Ruck was confused by the pronouncement, as he could still vividly remember the sight of her perfectly shaped legs as she ran toward her brother and he wondered how anyone could describe Magashi's legs as 'thick and lumpy'.

Puzzled but amused by the ridiculous nickname, Ruck let out a guffaw which caused Magashi to slap him playfully on the shoulder.

"It's not funny!" she admonished.

"No, no, it's not that I think your legs are cow

like, they are perfect!" Ruck protested, the improper declaration springing from his lips before he could think about what he was saying.

"Thank you," said Magashi quietly, blushing and turning back to her stew.

Mortified at his outburst, Ruck began to stammer an apology before he saw Magashi's eyes demurely rise to meet his. He decided to let the statement stand and the two young people settled into a comfortable silence, neither noticing the look of amusement on Kessay's face as he watched them from the corner of his eye.

Late that night after stowing his saddle and gear beneath one of the ramadas, Ruck entered the hut which he was to share with Kessay to find that Whitey had entered before him, and was already curled up on a blanket, fast asleep after a busy day. Kessay shook out his blanket to evict any multi-legged squatters and indicated that Ruck should do the same.

After a long, exhausting journey and having bellies full of good hot food, the men should have fallen asleep instantly but the two lay awake, having good reason for excitement.

"It is nice to be home, sometimes I wasn't sure I would ever see this place again" said Kessay.

"It's a good place, everyone seems happy to see

you," responded Ruck, thinking of one individual in particular "We never met your parents today, are they still around?"

"They passed away many years ago, when Magashi and I were very young. I provided for us after they died and I was very worried for my sister when they took me to the Territory" said Kessay.

"My parents are gone too," said Ruck "I did my best to take care of my sisters after they were gone, it seems like we have a lot in common."

"Do you ever miss your sisters?"

"No, they're married now, and they never seemed to have much use for me anyhow," said Ruck "You're lucky to have a sister like Magashi."

"She seems to like you," said Kessay.

"I like her too," replied Ruck.

"You shouldn't go off to the silver fields, Ruck. The people there are the same as the ones you say you were tired of back in Tennessee, and those outlaws might still be looking for you. We would make a place for you here, you would be happy" said Kessay.

Touched by the offer, Ruck pondered the thought of living among the Apache for long minutes. The thought of living in such a paradise with good friends was attractive, but conflicted with his desire to try his luck in the silver fields which had been his goal for a long time. To have come so far just to stop short of his original destination was an uncomfortable thought for Ruck, as the stubbornness which had driven him so far from home, now sought to drive him onward, despite the obvious fact that he could be happy here.

The issue remained unresolved in Ruck's mind as he finally drifted off to sleep, dreaming of lustrous black hair streaming in the wind.

The weather warmed dramatically over the next few weeks as spring gave way to summer and Ruck settled into a comfortable routine in the village. Knowing little of the Apache way of life, Ruck had much to learn, but he and Bolliver set about their work with a relentless drive that only a man raised on a farm and a Tennessee mule can muster, as they assisted the villagers with the myriad chores that were necessary for survival in the primitive village.

Though much work was done, Ruck spent many days hunting in the forest with Kessay and Bolliver or down by the river with Magashi learning the Apache language. Game was plentiful in the area, and Ruck put his father's old rifle to good use, bringing back deer, rabbits and even an elk which had been slow in leaving the lowlands where they spent the winter. The sojourns through the forest were enjoyable, but Ruck found himself looking forward to getting back to Whiteriver where he would butcher the game and clean the hides with Magashi as she taught him new words in the difficult to pronounce Apache language.

The oak trees, notoriously slow to bud were finally beginning to show some green when Kessay announced that the first dance of the year was drawing near, and asked Ruck to accompany him to Mr. Carter's trading post and purchase some supplies for the festival. Ruck readily agreed, and the two men loaded Bolliver with trade goods and set out on the thirty mile journey to the post. About half a mile from the village Whitey, not wanting to be left behind caught up with them and took his usual position in the vanguard.

After camping through the night, the men arrived at Carter's trading post about noon the next day. Carter himself was a man of middling height with a prodigious goatee and receding hairline with lines around his eyes from a habitual smile. The middle aged man greeted Kessay heartily, having heard from others that he had returned from exile in the Indian Territory and shook hands warmly with Ruck when introduced.

"So this is the white man who I hear is living in Whiteriver" said Carter not unkindly.

"Yessir, the N'dee have been very gracious hosts" said Ruck awkwardly pronouncing the unfamiliar Apache word.

"He even speaks the language!" Carter said in mock surprise "Why this fellow has gone native."

"More than you know Carter," said Kessay "He and Magashi seem to have come to an understanding."

Carter's surprise became real at the revelation and he shook Ruck's hand even more vigorously than before. "You lucked out son, there's not a better woman in this territory."

Embarrassed by the attention his romantic life was receiving, Ruck muttered his thanks stalling the conversation with his taciturn response.

The friendly Carter took the hint but was undaunted by Ruck's hesitation, and turned the conversation to business, bustling about as he filled Kessay's order, inspecting the goods that they had brought and negotiating shrewdly but fairly, finally arriving at a deal which was agreeable to both parties late in the afternoon. Being too late to start back toward Whiteriver, Carter invited Ruck and Kessay to stay the night and the two friends readily agreed.

"I hear that silver strike across the big canyon has turned out to be a big one" said Carter conversationally as they sat down to a meal of broiled steaks. "They say someone found a perfectly round silver nugget, and so they're going to name the town Globe."

"How far away is this?" asked Ruck, his interest piqued by talk of the silver fields he had dreamed of for so long.

"Oh, about fifty or sixty miles as the crow flies, but between here and there the Salt River cuts a mother of a canyon through the hills," said Carter "a fellow would do better to follow the Black River down into the flats and then turn north, unless that old mule of yours can fly."

"How far around that way then?" asked Ruck curiously.

"Couple of hundred miles I guess," replied Carter.

Knowing his friend's desire to try his luck in the silver fields, Kessay could almost read Ruck's mind as the three continued to eat in silence. He knew Ruck would want to see the town, if only for a sense of completion of his long journey, but Kessay wondered how Magashi would take it when she found out Ruck was leaving. She would want to go with him, Kessay decided, but the life of an Indian woman in a white boom town would not be a good one, and Kessay feared for both his sister and his friend if Ruck decided to strike out for Globe.

Kessay knew his friend well and his suppositions about Ruck's state of mind were correct, for as they spread their blankets on Carter's porch to sleep, the thought that the place he had dreamed of since he was a boy was within his grasp gnawed upon him. He did not relish the thought of leaving Magashi, but he had wanted to make it to the boom towns for so long that the idea just wouldn't quit. Torn between two courses of action, Ruck pondered long into the night as he watched Whitey's legs kick the air, as the dog chased rabbits through his dreams.

The men walked in silence for most of the next day, making their way back down the canyon toward Whiteriver. The still tension was broken by Kessay first when he could no longer watch his friend struggle alone.

"Magashi will not understand why you want to go to Globe," he said without preamble "Neither do I for that matter."

"I don't understand it well myself" replied Ruck, unsurprised at his friends insight "It's just that since I was a boy I've wanted to see the boom towns, maybe stake a claim and prosper, now there is a place just around the corner, if I don't go it will eat me up for the rest of my life, but if I do go I might lose you and Magashi and I can hardly bear to think about that."

"It's dangerous country, a lot of the boys around there are still fighting the cavalry and won't take kindly to a white man riding alone through their territory" Kessay warned "and speaking of cavalry, I can't go with you. I don't want to end up in the Territory again and I won't let Magashi go with you."

"I wouldn't ask you to," said Ruck "you've made

it home after being sent away once, and I would never ask you to leave it again."

"It could be your home too Ruck, just think about that,"

Ruck could not summon a reply and the men lapsed back into silence for the rest of the journey.

It was the day before the dance and a festive atmosphere pervaded the village but Magashi could not get into the spirit as she put the finishing touches on the dress she would wear. She had noticed a change in Ruck since he had come back from Carter's trading post, but neither Ruck nor her brother would confess what the problem was. Having little experience with men of her own people, much less white men, Magashi was in turmoil while she prepared her dress for the dance, wondering what she had done to cause the distance she sensed in Ruck's demeanor.

Her own fears and insecurities brought tears to her eyes as she worked, and the strength of her emotion brought her to the startling conclusion that she loved Alouicious Rucker. Picturing his silly hat with the creepy owl feather sticking out of it, she laughed through her tears at the strange choice her heart had made, but she knew that once the choice was made the will of the heart was irrevocable.

The Crown Dance was one of the most amazing things Ruck had ever witnessed. Huge bonfires were lit near the river and the whole village crowded into a circle to watch. Even the officers of the army camp and their wives were in attendance standing at a distance looking slightly uncomfortable as the men began to beat a steady rhythm on the drums and chant in an eerie wailing tone. Soon the dancers entered the firelight, the antler shaped crowns of their massive headdresses gleaming in the firelight, the feathers tied to their knees and elbows bobbing in time with the dancer's graceful steps.

Ruck and Magashi sat on a log holding hands as they watched the dancers spin and gyrate in time with the pounding of the drums. The rhythm was infectious and soon Ruck was tapping his toe in time with the beat. As entranced as he was, he was still distracted by thoughts of making the journey to the nearby boomtown, unconsciously comparing the rich beauty of the culture before him with the exciting image of the wild mining camp he had formed in his mind. As the tempo of the drums increased, the dancers matched the speed of the rhythm, their graceful movements reaching a crescendo as their performance drew encouraging whoops from the crowd.

Too soon, Ruck thought, the ritualistic performance was over, the exhausted dancers completing the intricate series of steps handed down for generations to herald the arrival of spring. This spring had not only brought the usual buds to the trees and fresh green shoots to the grass, but as it is wont to do, it caused the seeds of burgeoning romance to germinate within the soil of Ruck's heart producing the bittersweet shoots of new love. He was torn more than ever over whether to commit to a life with Magashi or to follow the dream he had had since he was a boy, but the sudden realization that to stay and remain torn was no option at all, and he knew with a sudden clarity that he must go, if only to drive the thought of prospecting from his mind forever. Steeling himself against his own doubt, he took Magashi's hand and led her away from the fires, and into the darkness. Kessay watched them as they disappeared into the shadows, lamenting what his sister and his best friend had to endure.

"I'm leaving for Globe in the morning" Ruck said simply in an attempt get the painful words out as quickly as possible.

Stunned, Magashi had no words with which to reply to the devastating blow she had received. The uncomfortable silence stretched to the point of agony before she found the strength to ask the only question she could:

"Why?"

"I've wanted to try my luck in the boom towns since I was a boy, I left my home in Tennessee to go to there, and now that I'm so close, I can't just give up on a dream I've had for so long" said Ruck, the words sounding trite in his ears even as he said them.

"Don't you like it here?" asked Magashi, her voice quavering with emotion.

"I love it here, but if I stay I'll always wonder if I made the wrong choice, I would always be troubled by my failure to reach the place I set out for" replied Ruck, staring up at the thick spangle of stars shining through the tops of the trees.

"Will you come back?" asked Magashi, grateful that the darkness concealed the tears streaming down her face.

"I don't know" said Ruck truthfully.

"I love you and I want you to stay," said Magashi putting her heart on the line with an all or nothing bid for the man she loved.

"I'm sorry Magashi, but I have to do this" said Ruck, wanting to say more but not trusting his voice to remain steady as he spoke the words which so devastated him.

Magashi turned and walked silently away, as the moon rose over the tops of the trees, shedding its argent light on a scene which it had illuminated many times before, that of two young hearts broken by the folly of a man's youthful dreams.

The next day Ruck saddled Bolliver before dawn, and bidding Kessay goodbye he mounted and followed the river to the south according to Carter's directions. Rather than feeling excitement at facing the final leg of his long journey, his heart was heavy with guilt and sorrow as he urged the mule into a trot, wishing the village to be out of sight before the sun rose fully and threatened to change his mind.

Bolliver could sense his friend's misery and did not understand why they were abandoning the best place they had found since leaving Tennessee, but the mule had resigned himself long ago to the fact that the motivations of man would ever remain a mystery to him and he dutifully carried Ruck away from what was clearly home.

Whitey ran alongside Bolliver, not ranging as far ahead as he usually did. The dog could sense something was wrong with Ruck and the mule, but he was too distracted by the fact that they seemed to be leaving the village to try to find out what the matter was. Every few hundred yards Whitey would pause in his normal investigations of the surrounding countryside to look back up the canyon where he could smell the smoke from the morning fires as they were banked up to prepare breakfast.

Noticing that Whitey kept looking back the way toward the village, Ruck smiled bitterly.

"I know how you feel, Whitey" he said.

Chapter 16

Lacking the tracking abilities of an army scout or Indian, I followed Rucker's trail the only way I knew how, by asking questions of the people I met. The problem with gathering information in the manner of a big city reporter was that in the sparsely populated west, there were few people to inquire of. But I persevered, knowing that Rucker must be forewarned of the murderers who sought him.

--excerpt from 'In Pursuit of a Legend, a Memoir' by Peabody Samuelson

Peabody rode south at a brisk pace, following the clearly defined cattle trails, hoping to cross paths with someone who had seen or heard of Alouicious Rucker. Now that Sunshine had learned to respect Peabody, the horse loped along at a smooth gait which did not jar his injured shoulder overmuch, and the miles seemed to fly beneath the hooves of the tireless cowpony.

They overtook a stagecoach the first afternoon, but the neither the passengers nor the driver had heard of Rucker or Beckwith and after a short conversation, Peabody urged Sunshine back to a lope once more. Finally making camp after a tremendous day of riding, Peabody combed and fed Sunshine before inspecting the bandages on his wounded chest and shoulder. The wound did not seem to have reopened during the frantic ride, and Peabody doubted his ability to keep it clean while on the trail, so he left the bandages in place, and lay down on his bedroll quickly falling fast asleep.

While breaking his fast the next morning, Peabody reassessed the grueling pace he had set for Sunshine, considering it might be days or weeks before he caught up to Rucker, if ever. There was no doubt in Peabody's mind that the stalwart little cowpony would run until he foundered if Peabody asked him to, but Sunshine had become dear to the man and Peabody would not demand such a great sacrifice from the horse.

The easier pace they set the next day allowed Peabody much time for reflection, as the terrain along the cattle trail was featureless save for the occasional mountain standing blue and indistinct in the hazy distance. Peabody was troubled as he somehow felt responsible for the outlaw's pursuit of Rucker though he couldn't put his finger on why. Maybe the articles he had written for the newspaper, which according to the telegraphs Peabody had received from Mr. Johnson had been reprinted a number of times by popular demand, had been too much for the proud outlaw to bear. But it was also possible that Rucker and Beckwith had known each other long before their encounter in Memphis, maybe the vendetta was the result of an older feud which the capture of Logan was only an extension.

As the miles rolled by, Peabody's analytical mind speculated endlessly over the reasons why Logan might pursue Rucker over such a vast distance, but his normally focused mind kept turning away from the topic as he thought of his beloved Eunice. Doubt about the wisdom of his course of action assailed Peabody as he considered the fact that he had already been shot once, and now he was traveling through a vast dangerous country, endeavoring to warn a man he had never met of a threat which might never materialize. Already he had gone far beyond the call of duty to find and interview Rucker, and the sane thing for any man to do at this point would be to turn Sunshine back toward Cimarron and settle into a quiet life with Eunice, finishing his book. Despite the obvious allure of turning back, Peabody urged Sunshine into a trot, scanning the horizon for any sign of another human being, hoping to hear some word of Alouicious Rucker.

The plains of the New Mexico Territory gradually turned to desert as Peabody made his way south, with short grass and cedar trees giving way to sand and mesquite bushes. Water became hard to come by in the arid land, and Peabody began to grow worried until he spied a verdant valley which cut through the landscape like a green ribbon in the distance. Relieved, Peabody allowed Sunshine to deviate to the west from the southerly route they had followed so far. Soon they arrived at the banks of a shallow muddy river, quenching their thirst eagerly and resting beneath the shade of the sparse trees which grew along the banks.

Idly resting while Sunshine cropped the succulent grass, Peabody's gaze drifted across the bare sandy hills which stretched to the horizon. A dust devil twisted its way lazily through the sand in the distance, and Peabody spotted its twin rising from the desert floor farther to the south. Sleepily watching the two dust devils come closer together, Peabody noted a difference in the two clouds. The first was tall and stately, swaying only a little as it danced along the dunes, but the second seemed to hang low to the ground, drifting up slowly like smoke from a fire. Peabody's mind latched on to the incongruity in the two desert phenomena, his sleep deprived mind struggling to identify the reason the second disturbance seemed odd. Like lightning, the thought stuck Peabody that the second cloud was no dust devil at all but the cloud caused by a group of horses or a wagon disturbing the dust of the trail. Jumping to his feet, Peabody grabbed up his shotgun and mounted Sunshine, who reluctantly turned away from his repast and broke into a gallop on a line to intercept the travelers.

As Peabody approached the trail, he soon discovered that the source of the dust cloud was a stagecoach making its way north along the cattle trail which Peabody had followed for days. Not wanting to cause a tragic misunderstanding, Peabody kept his shotgun in the saddle scabbard and raised his hand to hail the stage.

The teamster pulled on the reins halting the coach and the elderly man seated beside him held a shotgun at the ready, wary of lone riders along such a wild trail.

"Howdy," called Peabody, carefully keeping his hands in view "Could you tell me how far it is to the nearest town?"

"Mesilla is about twenty miles back that way" responded the old man riding shotgun "You can follow the river, it will take you right into town."

"Much obliged," said Peabody gratefully "I'm looking for a man named Alouicious Rucker, maybe you've heard of him, there's some bad men after him and he's got to be warned, he could be around here but he might have turned west into the Arizona Territory"

"I can't say as I have ever met anyone named of Alouicious," said the teamster incredulously.

"Didn't that bunch of soldiers from Camp Apache say there was a white man who had gone native in the hills above the Black River?" the old man said "What did they say his name was?"

"I don't recall them giving a name, but if he fell in with the Apache he'll be dead as a doornail by now" said the teamster.

"Sorry we couldn't be more help youngster, but the soldiers should still be hanging around Mesilla or El Paso, and if anybody has heard of your man it will be those boys"

"Thanks again old timer," said Peabody as he hurriedly turned Sunshine to the south, goading the horse into a gallop, hoping to catch the soldiers before they moved on.

Mesilla was a sleepy little pueblo on the banks of the Rio Grande River near the Texas border, but compared to the quiet empty lands Peabody had just passed through it seemed to bustle with activity as people went to and fro about their evening tasks. Whitewashed adobe buildings were scattered along both sides of the riverbank, and numerous people were in evidence as they moved about the dusty little village.

To the west, the setting sun painted the sparsely clouded sky in vibrant tones of pink and gold in a magnificent display that was unlike anything Peabody had ever seen, and to the east, a mountain of bare rock jutted from the desert floor like a massive stone rampart. So tall and steep was the bladelike protrusion that it brought to mind the pipes of a colossal church organ. Peabody absorbed the majestic view in wonder for long minutes, before gently urging Sunshine toward the village.

Despite the fact that Mesilla seemed to have a dearth of people who spoke English, Peabody quickly found the saloon, which by now Peabody had discovered was the societal and cultural hub of nearly every town west of the Mississippi. After securing lodging for Sunshine in the nearby livery stable, he entered the crowded saloon and made his way through the clouds of tobacco smoke and press of bodies to the bar. Peabody ordered a beer but none was available, and he passed on the offer of rye whiskey which to his mind was a poor way to wash the trail dust from one's throat. He accepted a glass of soda water much to the barkeep's dismay and inquired about the soldiers that the old man on the stagecoach had said might still be in town. Wanting to make room at the crowded bar for someone who might order more than soda water, the bartender quickly indicated a rough looking, unshaven fellow who sat in a corner conversing with a heavyset Mexican woman. Peabody offered his thanks and worked his way around the tables toward the wild looking man.

"Good evening sir, might I have a word?" said Peabody as he arrived at the man's table.

"What can I do for you cowpoke?" asked the man gruffly. He was wearing a fringed buckskin jacket which was mostly black with dirt and grease, and a hat that looked like it had not had a furlough since Manassas. Several days' growth of patchy salt and pepper beard struggled to cover the man's weak chin and pockmarked cheeks.

"My name is Peabody Samuelson, and I'm looking for a unit of soldiers who I was told came this way recently," he said "the bartender referred me to you."

"I'm William Lilley, scout attached to Fort Bowie, at your service" said the man proudly "what do you need soldiers for, Mr. Samuelson?"

"Well it's not exactly the soldiers I am interested in," replied Peabody "I am trying to find a man who may have gone this direction recently, and I thought the army might have word of him."

"Does he owe you money or something?" asked William.

"No, nothing like that" said Peabody hurriedly, "there is a bad outlaw on his trail and I wish to warn him of the danger his is in."

"Is he a friend of yours then?"

"Not exactly, we haven't met," said Peabody, growing frantic in an attempt to explain his reasons for trailing a man halfway across the country "I'm a reporter you see, and I've been trying to find Rucker for some time so I can interview him for my newspaper. In Santa Fe I ran afoul of the outlaw who is looking for him and now I have to find him before he gets killed."

"Did you say Rucker?" asked the scout thoughtfully.

"Why yes I did, Alouicious Rucker is his name" said Peabody hopefully "Have you seen him?"

"I haven't seen him myself, but I heard awhile back about a white man named Rucker who had taken up with the White Mountain Apaches, I imagine that's him" said William simply.

"Where do these White Mountain Apache live?" asked Peabody, elated to finally find word of Rucker.

"Oh, northeast of here in the Arizona Territory, but it's a wild country between here and there, you wouldn't have a snowball's chance in Hades of making it there alone" explained the scout.

Discouraged by the pronouncement, Peabody let out a slow breath, "I've come too far to stop now, and I must try to reach him" he said.

"I'm leaving for Fort Bowie in the morning, you can ride along with me that far, after that I imagine you can catch one of the units headed toward Camp Apache, there's bound to be one before long" said the scout taking pity on Peabody.

"Much obliged Mr. Lilley, I will" said Peabody, his hope springing anew "How can I ever repay you?"

"Another whiskey would be nice, and after that a little privacy" said William nodding toward the woman who had waited patiently while the conversation wound on.

Ebullient, Peabody pushed his chair back and stood up and moved toward the bar to buy the man a drink, hot on the trail of a legend once again.

The next morning Peabody was up before the sun, his shoulder was still a little stiff, but the wound showed no sign of infection and seemed to be healing nicely. Eager to be on his way, Peabody packed his few things and as the sun was peeking over the rugged stone of the jutting mountain range he went to the telegraph office to send a report to Mr. Johnson. After giving a short account of Rucker's recovery and the subsequent reports of his having taken up with the Apache, Peabody added a post script to the message, inquiring about the possibility of compiling the numerous stories he had written about Rucker into a short novel. Completing the telegraph to his editor, Peabody also sent one to Eunice, apprising her of his progress and assuring her that he would be back as soon as he could. Peabody hoped that he was nearing the end of his odyssey, wanting nothing more than to finish his assignment and head back to Cimarron to see the McCall ranch and Eunice once again.

When Peabody arrived at the stable to collect Sunshine, the horse seemed to be in high spirits, greeting his friend with a boisterous neigh. Peabody quickly found out the reason for Sunshine's good humor, and having to pay the livery owner extra due to the hoof shaped bruise on the man's backside. Peabody saddled Sunshine himself to avoid further incident and Sunshine drank his fill when led to the trough, as though understanding there was a long, dry road ahead. While Sunshine was still drinking, William arrived at the stable to collect his own mount, and Peabody was surprised to see the scout emerge from the barn with a pony quite like his own.

"That Indian pony will do real well where we're going, I was afraid you would have one of those big thoroughbreds they prefer back east" said William casting an appraising eye on Sunshine.

"Why thank you," replied Peabody "he seems to do quite well, but he's very spirited, I would stand well clear of his back hooves if you don't want a kick."

"He must be kin to this nag I ride" said William, the fondness in his eyes when he looked at his horse giving lie to the harsh words the scout used to describe the horse. "Well I guess we better get going, it's a long ride to Fort Bowie."

Peabody mounted without reply and the two men turned their small steeds to the west, quickly leaving the sleepy village behind them.

Both the weather and the company were pleasant as the two rode through the grasslands. Besides the ubiquitous buzzards the only sign of life on the plain were the antelope which occasionally approached to within a few hundred yards of the men before trotting off to be lost in the distance. Having no geographical features to circumvent, the scout set a course which never deviated, but still brought them with unerring precision to the few sources of water between Mesilla and Fort Bowie.

William proved to be a pleasant traveling companion, telling hair-raising tales of his service with the cavalry, and prompting Peabody for news from the east, where he hadn't been since the war and the two filled the many miles trading stories back and forth making an otherwise interminable journey pleasant and entertaining.

As the days passed, the two men became good friends, and it was with some lament that the two arrived at Fort Bowie to find that their paths had to separate. William received orders to stay at the Fort to await the arrival of a company of infantry who were in the field and had lost their scout, while Peabody was able to join a company of cavalry who were leaving the same afternoon for Camp Apache. Peabody and William shook hands in a warm farewell and soon Peabody was on his way north, following the cavalry, trying with little success to avoid the prodigious dust kicked up by the army horses.

The journey north, while not as entertaining without William, was beautiful, as the relentless flatness of the landscape slowly gave way to rolling hills and steep bluffs. Tall cactus with arms pointed toward the sky began to appear, and soon the massive succulents dotted the surrounding hills making Peabody think that soon they would be traveling through a forest of the towering green sentinels. Tiny deer and grayish pig-like creatures which the soldiers identified as javelina moved amongst the cactus and mesquite bushes eking out a living from the arid landscape.

As the days fled, juniper and cedar trees began to appear among the steep ridges and hills and soon the column came in sight of the first river they had seen for what seemed to Peabody to be an eternity. The officers at the front of the column drew up well short of the river and seemed to be conferring with a scout, though Peabody was too far away to hear what was being said. The conference seemed to come to a conclusion and the soon column was moving forward again.

As Peabody approached the river, he noticed a man riding a mule toward the column of soldiers. Thinking that this stranger was what the scout had been discussing with the officers, Peabody studied the man who seemed to be following the river and was followed closely by what appeared to be a shaggy dog. The man soon arrived among the soldiers who had stopped their horses to water along the river. Peabody wondered what any lone white man was doing traveling through Apache country and moved Sunshine closer to the man thinking he might have heard of Alouicious Rucker.

"Howdy," Peabody hailed, having grown accustom to using the western expression.

"Hello," replied the overall clad man, seeming to be in no mood for conversation.

"My name is Peabody Samuelson," continued the reporter, undaunted by the man's curt manner "I wonder if I might have a word?"

The man seemed to realize he was being rude and drew his mule to a stop but his bearded face still showed signs of great sorrow as he turned toward Peabody "I'm Alouicious Rucker, what can I do for you, Mr. Samuelson?"

"Rucker?" said Peabody in a small voice, before letting out a triumphant shout which startled all who heard it, man and beast.

Chapter 17

When words are many, transgression is not lacking. But whoever restrains his lips is prudent.

Proverbs 10:19

     Abel Beckwith let out a relieved sigh as the three outlaws finally came into sight of Silver City. When they had left Tennessee, Abel had had only a vague conception of what the west was like, but the descriptions he had heard over many card tables had not prepared him for the reality of the vast, sparsely settled region. The outlaws had avoided contact with people fearing posses and Indians as they crossed the breadth of the Indian Territory, and nearly bisected New Mexico, and with the exception of short stops at Fort Bascom and Santa Fe, the men had not seen enough people to fill a stage coach. Abel glanced up at a large bird wheeling through the skies overhead, and though he knew the thought to be ridiculous, he could not shake the feeling that the same buzzard had followed them since they crossed the Arkansas River, weeks before.

     Now though, a bustling boom town lay before

them, with rough plank shacks, tents and even a few stone buildings scattered amongst the cedar trees, and Abel could only hope they had enough time to get clean and properly fed before his brother did something foolish and they were on the run again.

After Logan had shot the reporter, and over the course of their sojourn through the wind scoured prairies, Abel had given much thought to turning his brother in to the first lawman they met, and riding away without looking back. But the thoughts had been idle ones as the miles of grassland fled beneath the hooves of their mounts, since they happened across no one, law or otherwise.

"Logan, I know it's an inconvenience but could you kindly try not to shoot anyone until I've had time to finish a small glass of whiskey?" asked Jean-Batiste, echoing Abel's thoughts.

"Very funny, Le'Chiffre," replied Logan sarcastically.

"Are we going into town or are we going to sit here and bicker all day?" asked Abel, nudging his horse forward and heading toward the town.

The tired and irritable trio made their way down the ridge and into town which was situated in a narrow valley among the steep hills. The livery stable was little more than a corral with some stacks of hay and a crude water trough, but the three gladly paid the exorbitant mining town fees, grateful to have a chance to be off of the saddles which had been their home for far too long.

In true boom town fashion every other structure seemed to be a saloon, gambling hall or both, and Logan headed straight for a nearby shack with a crudely painted sign proclaiming it to be the 'Gold Dust Saloon.'

"I might see if there's a barber with a bathtub in this town," said Abel, pausing and looking up the street.

"A shave might make me feel like a human being again, I think I'll join you" said Jean-Batiste.

"You ladies don't get lost now," said Logan over his shoulder, as he entered the saloon.

The barber turned out to be a middle aged Mexican man who offered grooming and some light dentistry from a collection of tents near the center of town. The bathtub was just a horse trough, but Able had had enough of the feel of powdery dust glued to him by his own sweat and gladly stepped behind the hanging sheet which acted as a screen, doffing his clothes and lowering himself into the lukewarm water.

Waiting his turn in the tub, Jean-Batiste asked the barber for a shave and as the man lathered his chin, Le'Chiffre could hear the sloshing of the water behind the curtain.

"What do you think our chances are of being able to stay around here a while Abel?" said Jean-Batiste, trying to talk without moving his jaw as the barber began to scrape the stubble from his chin.

"I guess it depends on whether Logan gets word of Rucker or that Indian," replied Abel as he scrubbed his face and neck furiously. "If he does, we'll be after them again; Logan ain't one to forgive someone who he thinks made a fool of him."

"If he does hear about them do you think we could stay here and let him go after them alone? This town seems to have potential for men like us" asked Le'Chiffre.

"If we try to split from Logan, he will shoot us and leave us for the buzzards," replied Abel matter-of-factly "Logan was always the leader of any gang he was with, he thinks of any disagreement as disloyalty, and as soon as he thinks you're disloyal you are a dead man. I wish we could stay here just as much as you do, but we're stuck with him until he takes care of Rucker."

"Or someone takes care of Logan," said Le'Chiffre thoughtfully.

"What was that?" asked Abel, rinsing the soap from his ears.

"Oh, nothing, just thanking this fine gentleman for the shave," replied Jean-Batiste using a towel to wipe the remaining lather from his face.

Sheriff Harry Drake was rarely found in his office, as the monumental task of policing a wild frontier town like Silver City left little time for idleness, but every action he took to clean up Grant county resulted in an equal measure of paperwork and it was this onerous task that the sheriff applied himself to as the barber entered and humbly removed his floppy cap.

"Ah, Mr. Medina," greeted Sheriff Drake, "what brings you here this morning?" Sheriff Drake was a man of medium height and slim build, with streaks of grey through his black hair which gave him a distinguished look. He wore a plain suit while at the office, but the sweat stained, dusty hat hanging on a rack near the door bore testament to the many hours he spent on the trail enforcing the law in the boom town.

"Good Morning Sheriff," replied Medina "I wonder if I might have a word with you." Ricardo Medina's barber shop had been one of the first businesses established in the area after the discovery of a rich silver lode brought prospectors from all over the country to try their luck. A portly, unassuming man, Medina had done quite well for himself, providing services to the miners, teamsters and assorted ruffians who populated the area, but his work, innocuous as it was, had been fraught with danger due to the lawless nature of the burgeoning town. Ricardo had seen that start to change when Sheriff Drake had been elected the previous year, and thus the barber was grateful to the tough Sheriff and wished to do his part in keeping his community safe from outlaws and brigands. Being in the service industry, and a Mexican to boot, rendered Ricardo virtually invisible to most of his white customers, and he used the phenomenon to his advantage, providing the Sheriff with any information he came across in the course of his work.

"Some men came by for a bath and a shave awhile ago, and they said some things that made me think they might be up to no good" said the barber, taking a seat across the desk from the Sheriff.

"Like what?" asked Sheriff Drake. Over the last few months Medina had proved to be an excellent source of information, and the Sheriff was often surprised by the things people let slip when they were in the barber's chair.

"Two men were at my place, speaking about another," replied the barber "Both men were armed, one had a pistol, and the other carried a shotgun, they seemed to have been on the road for a long time and I got the impression they were after someone named 'Rucker.' The two men seemed to have grown tired of the chase and wanted to stay here in town for a while, but they seemed to think that the third would kill them if they did not follow when he left."

"Sounds like a rough bunch, but that's not quite

enough to arrest them," said Drake "did you get their names?"

"I didn't ask their names, I didn't want to arouse suspicion, but during the conversation they referred to the third man simply as Logan" said Ricardo.

The name struck a familiar chord with the Sheriff and he rifled through the papers on his desk until he found what he was looking for. It was a telegraph he had received from the U.S. marshal's office in El Paso advising him to be on the lookout for a man named Logan Beckwith who had shot a reporter in Santa Fe. The telegraph had been thorough, describing Beckwith as a large, dark haired man in his middle thirties with a thick beard. Unfortunately, that described roughly a third the men in Silver City, but the telegraph did mention the possibility that Beckwith was traveling with two companions.

"Where are these men now?" the Sheriff asked Medina rising from his chair and buckling on his pistol.

"I watched them as long as I could, without being conspicuous," replied Ricardo "they looked like they were headed for The Gold Dust."

"Thanks Ricardo," said the Sheriff as he retrieved his hat and made for the door, "I'll let you know how it turns out."

Jean-Batiste and Abel felt comfortable for the

first time in what seemed like ages as after bathing and eating a satisfying lunch they settled down to a game of cards with some of the prospectors in The Gold Dust Saloon.

They had each taken a few hands, playing conservatively until they could gauge the measure of their opponents, and the two quickly became engrossed in the game after such a long absence from civilization. Thus it was that they didn't notice the three men approaching the table until one of them spoke:

"I'd like to have a word with you two if I could" said Sheriff Drake, easily picking out the two freshly bathed and shaved men from among the ill kempt patrons of the Gold Dust. Drake felt confident that he and the two deputies he had brought with him had the drop on the two suspicious men and hoped to avoid armed confrontation in the crowded saloon.

"Why of course Sheriff," replied Le'Chiffre reading the brass badge pinned to Drake's chest and offering his best winning smile.

"Where's your partner Logan?" asked Drake with his hand on the butt of his pistol.

Other, more flamboyant villains might have quipped something like 'right behind you, Lawman' giving the Sheriff and his men time to react to his presence, but Logan simply drew his pistol and fired repeatedly at the officers' backs, fanning the hammer on his revolver and sending bullets flying wildly through the room.

Pandemonium ensued in the saloon as Logan emptied his gun into the lawmen, Abel and Jean-Batiste ducked and covered their heads as bullets whizzed around them. The other patrons of the saloon scattered, heading for an exit or taking cover as flame and smoke billowed forth from the muzzle of Logan's revolver. The sheriff and his two deputies fell to the dirt floor as Logan calmly replaced his pistol in his holster and grabbed a bottle of whiskey as he turned for the door.

"Well boys, I guess I've had enough of Silver City, let's go" said Logan.

Recovering quickly from the sudden violence, Abel and Jean-Batiste quickly followed Logan out the door, Le'Chiffre having the presence of mind to gather the money which still lay in the center of the table before they hastily made their exit, stepping over the still bodies of the men Logan had shot.

Emerging from the saloon, the outlaws untied the three best looking horses from the hitching rail and mounted, spurring the stolen steeds mercilessly toward the edge of town. As the three desperados galloped into the wilderness, Abel realized that Jean-Batiste's dire predictions had come to pass, as many people who were in the Gold Dust would surely be able to recognize them and Logan's actions made them accessories to the murder of a lawman and horse thieves to boot, both of which were hanging offenses. Any hopes Abel had of parting ways with his maniacal brother were dashed now as their fates were hopelessly intertwined and as Abel resigned himself to a life on the run, he wondered what the weather was like in Mexico this time of year.

Jean-Batiste was furious with himself for not separating himself from Logan long ago, and now it seemed to be too late, as surely there would shortly be a posse on their trail. As Logan turned his horse to the northeast, the thought occurred to Le'Chiffre that they would wish for the hangman's noose if they ran afoul of any renegade Indians in the rugged country where they were headed. They had been lucky to avoid any hostile Indians so far, but as they rode farther west their luck was sure to run out eventually.

Logan gave none of these matters a thought as he goaded the stolen horse to greater speed, taking his shooting of three lawmen as a matter of course in his search for revenge against those he thought had brought about his ruin. Posses had always been an occupational hazard for Logan, and even in unfamiliar territory he had full confidence in his ability to evade pursuit. The short sighted desperado gave no thought anything beyond the destruction of his enemies.

The thee outlaws set a varying pace to husband the strength of the horses they had stolen, and the route they took to the northwest was circuitous not only to throw off pursuit by the posse that was sure to be on their trail, but to negotiate the mountains which seemed to grow more rugged by the hour. Silver City was situated in an area where the vast arid plains abruptly transitioned to the high country along the New Mexico Arizona border. Deep canyons cut across their path, and precipitous mesas rose about them causing the men to backtrack and change directions repeatedly. Cedar, live oak and pine trees mingled together, stubbornly clinging to nearly vertical slopes. Soon the men were dismounting regularly, leading their horses up or down the more prodigious grades, picking their way along switchback paths to the top of a ridge, only to discover that another steep slope greeted them on the other side.

Late in the evening, rain began to fall and exhausted and unwilling to risk injury in the treacherous footing of the rugged country in the dark, the outlaws made a cold camp near the bottom of a canyon as twilight descended huddling beneath the branches of a small pine tree as the cold rain fell steadily.

"Small wonder the army has trouble keeping the Indians corralled in this part of the country," said Abel, looking at the slopes rising around them in the rapidly failing light, "a million people could be camping one ridge over and you'd play hell finding them."

The casual observation gave the men pause, as

all three considered the possibility that the rocky buttes and ridges surrounding them could conceal any number of Indians or lawmen and there would be no way to know about them until it was too late.

The storm continued through the night, and despite their weariness, the men slept fitfully, uncomfortable on the wet pine needles and repeatedly awakened by the peal of thunder. After an interminable night, the men awoke groggily to find their mounts had disappeared. Before they had settled in to their dubious shelter Logan had made sure the horses had been hobbled, but as the sky brightened with the first rays of dawn, neither horse nor hobble was in evidence. The continual rain throughout the night had washed away any trace of what might have occurred, and the men found themselves stranded on foot, deep in Indian country.

"It had to be Indians," said Abel casting his gaze along the ridgelines surrounding them.

"If it was Indians why did they leave us alone? It's not as if they didn't see us, the horses were only a few yards away" said Le'Chiffre.

"It must have been just one or two youngsters," replied Logan "If it had been a big group we would be dead as doornails right now."

"Since when are you the world's authority on Indians?" asked an irritated Abel.

"It's common knowledge you insolent whelp" said Logan through gritted teeth as he narrowed his gaze at his brother.

"It doesn't matter where the horses went," interjected Jean-Batiste, trying to diffuse the tense situation "we should get going. We have a long walk ahead of us, and who knows when whoever took the horses might be back."

The Beckwith brothers continued to scowl at each other, as the men gathered what few supplies they had left and set out on foot, each of them looking and listening intently for any sign of a pursuing posse or roving Indians.

It was a ragged and weary trio who arrived in town days later, all three men limped on ankles twisted by the steep, rocky terrain and their clothes were filthy tatters after the harrowing ordeal they had endured. What little game the outlaws had taken and the sparse ground water available had served to keep them alive, but the prolonged exposure coupled with long daily marches through the rugged country had sapped most of the outlaw's strength. After cresting a seemingly endless series of ridgelines and circumnavigating numerous steep canyons, the men had finally come across a road and followed it north where it led them to what appeared to be nothing more than a mining camp, newer and even more primitive than even Silver City had been. Though exhausted and near death, the desperados had the presence of mind to give false names to the kindly people who gathered about to provide succor to the bedraggled men who stumbled into the camp.

After drinking deeply from a canteen offered by one of the prospectors, Abel asked a question that swam incongruously to the front of his addled mind.

"Where are we?" he croaked through parched lips.

"Just a new mining camp," replied the friendly prospector "we call it Globe."

Chapter 18

During the long weeks of my quest to find Alouicious Rucker I had spent many a long hour trying to imagine what he was like, but when I finally met him I found that even my wildest imaginings had not come close to the reality of the man.

--excerpt from 'In Pursuit of a Legend, a Memoir' by Peabody Samuelson

"So you never actually laid a hand on Beckwith when he was captured back in Tennessee?" Peabody asked Ruck as the two sat near a campfire near the banks of the Black River. The men had set a small camp a short distance away from that of the company of soldiers who Peabody had traveled with since leaving Fort Bowie.

"I tried to help him up after he fell off his horse, but I didn't knock him down if that's what you're asking" replied Ruck. Since the two men had met a few hours before, Ruck had been dismayed and a little puzzled to discover that a reporter had followed him all the way from Memphis simply to interview him about his adventures since leaving Tennessee. The events that Peabody seemed so interested in were admittedly amusing at times, but hardly seemed newsworthy to Ruck, as he thought back to the accidents and mishaps which had occurred in his travels.

"And is this the same dog that you taught to spot a card cheat?" asked Peabody, indicating Whitey who was lying at Ruck's side trying with little success to digest a rabbit that had been a half step too slow.

"I don't think you could teach this dog anything," said Ruck chuckling as he scratched Whitey behind the ears affectionately "that cheating rascal on the boat was just feeding him jerky from the same pocket where he was rat-holing high cards, and when Whitey dug in that pocket to get more he came up with an ace, then all hell broke loose."

Peabody laughed out loud at both the antics of the dog and his own folly at going to such lengths to track down a story which was nothing more than a series of incredible mishaps.

"I have to admit, the true story of what happened is much funnier than any of the stories I've heard about you," said Peabody, "but I guess Logan Beckwith didn't find them all that funny" he continued suddenly sobering.

"A friend of mine said they were after me, I sure never meant to cause as much trouble as I have" said

Ruck "like you said, it was all just an accident that I ever even met the men."

"Hearing you tell the story, it's hard to imagine why they have gone to such lengths to find you, but there's no accounting for the actions of a crazy man" said Peabody shuddering at the memory of the cold look in Logan's eyes when he had pulled the trigger back in Santa Fe. "Where have you been since you left Santa Fe? You seemed to drop off the face of the earth for quite a while" said the reporter changing the subject.

"I met up with an old boy who guided me through the New Mexico territory, and for a while I've been staying back in those hills with his people" replied Ruck.

"His people? You mean the Apache?" asked Peabody.

"Yes," replied Ruck simply, not meeting Peabody's eyes.

Peabody could sense Ruck's discomfort at the mention of the people he had lived with, but could not discern its source and despite his journalistic instinct, Peabody elected to let the matter lie until Ruck was ready to divulge the details of his life among the Indians.

"What do you think of the west so far?"

Peabody asked to lighten the suddenly somber mood "I find that it agrees with me, and I may stick around once I send my promised article to my editor."

Ruck considered the question for long moments, thinking back over the weeks since he had left home. "Ever since I was a boy I've wanted to go west," he said finally "I had this picture in my head of what it would be like, but now that I'm here its much different than I ever imagined. In some ways it is not what I hoped it would be, but in others it's better than I ever dreamed. I'm glad I came."

Peabody smiled at the frank admission "Growing up in the city I was always a little afraid of the wilderness, but now that I'm here I don't think I'll go back to Memphis. I've had to endure things out here I never would have thought possible back home, but if I accept these wild places on their own terms, I discover parts of myself I never knew existed."

At that the two men fell into silence, lost in their own thoughts until the fire burned low and sleep overtook them.

Well before dawn the next morning, Peabody and Ruck were awakened by the sounds of the nearby soldiers making ready to continue their journey to Camp Apache and rose themselves to fumble about in the dark trying with some difficulty to saddle Bolliver and Sunshine by starlight.

"I'll never understand why the army insists on waking up in the middle of the night" said Peabody as he tried to secure the cinch on Sunshine's saddle by feel.

"My Pa always said he never shot any game in the dark" said Ruck "I can't imagine what these boys think they will accomplish before daylight."

After some struggle the two men had their mounts ready to go just as the column of soldiers was leaving camp singing the familiar refrain of 'The Girl I left Behind Me.' The lyrics of the ubiquitous army tune caused Ruck to think of Magashi and as the cavalry unit headed east just as the sky was beginning to brighten, Ruck gave serious thought to mounting Bolliver and following along with them, but sheer youthful stubbornness prevailed and he mounted the mule and sat waiting for the reporter to saddle up.

Peabody too was affected by the song which spoke of such lament, and thoughts of Eunice so far away combined with his sleep deprived state to stir bitterness in his heart. Peabody had tracked a man he thought was a hero across the entire New Mexico territory and into Arizona, only to find that his quarry was in actuality an unassuming hillbilly riding a mule. Any book that he might write about this man would be either a tissue of lies or a dismal failure, possibly both. Maybe he could find a job with the newspaper in Cimarron, if there was one, he thought. If not, he could start one, and maybe eke out a good enough living to provide for Eunice. Wanting only to reach Globe, where he planned to re-provision and rest up for the long trip back to his beloved Eunice, Peabody angrily gained the saddle and urged Sunshine into a trot heading north with Ruck and Bolliver quickly falling in beside them.

Both men were lost in gloomy introspection throughout the day, with a disillusioned Peabody wallowing in self pity over what he considered the world's greatest fool's errand, and Ruck sullen over his own stubborn refusal to forgo the dubious pleasure of prospecting among the desolate hills. The day passed in relative silence, the beautiful spring weather contrasting sharply with the two men's dark moods. The men rode hard, stopping infrequently but it was still late afternoon before the men reached the mining camp.

Ruck had maintained the mental image of the boom towns that he had had since he was a child, sitting at the hearth, listening to Almer's tales of the excitement and bustle of the camps. The thrill of fortunes won and lost in a day, wild gamblers and sporting women plying their respective trades among the grizzled prospectors who were continually striking vast lodes of precious metals in the rich silver fields of the southwest had been the spur which goaded him to leave Tennessee and head west. Needless to say, Ruck was disappointed by his first sight of Globe.

Tents and ramshackle structures were scattered

about the rocky valley in a haphazard fashion and the detritus of humanity was in evidence everywhere in the form of grimy, desperate prospectors, miners, and mule skinners. Any trees that had been in the area had been cut down in a wide swath around the collection of makeshift shelters, and piles of rock spoil stood alongside great gashes in the earth where men had dug in apparently random locations seeking silver. A pall of smoke hung over the wretched scene robbing the area of even the fresh air and sunshine which was abundant just a few short miles away.

Ruck muttered an uncharacteristic oath as he took in the dismal sight before him, and as the depth of his folly finally became clear to him his youthful stubbornness crumbled and he was tempted to turn Bolliver around right then and there and head back for Whiteriver.

"What a delightful little community, I bet the shops along the boardwalk are just lovely" said Peabody sarcastically as he nudged Sunshine toward the camp.

Ruck chuckled, as Peabody's joke broke the spell his despair had cast over him and urged Bolliver to follow. Whitey seemed unsure of why the men were going to such a rotten smelling place, but Ruck had not steered them wrong so far and the faithful cur reluctantly followed along.

Following their difficult journey through the

mountains, Jean-Batiste and the Beckwith brothers took their time recuperating in Globe. The mining camp could hardly be called a town, having been started only a few months earlier, but the discovery of pay dirt had caused prospectors and miners to flock to the encampment in droves. So new was the burgeoning community that so far only those who wished to find silver had arrived, and before the outlaws came to the camp it had been free of the gamblers, conmen and loose women who would inevitably follow the prospectors into the area. Another attractive feature of the newborn community was the complete absence of law. Since the outlaws had been in town, no one had even mentioned the shooting of the sheriff in New Mexico much less come looking for them.

Thus Jean-Batiste and Abel found themselves free of pursuit and in virgin territory and had quickly taken advantage of the fact, starting up an almost continuous poker game in which the two men so badly outclassed their opponents they hardly had to cheat at all. The men had quickly trimmed enough money off of the hapless miners so that they were able to purchase a large tent from a prospector who was down on his luck which they then pitched near the center of the scattered claims. Setting up two tables inside, they soon had a place where the miners could stop by any time and give their hard earned money away.

Logan spent the time sulking over his lost love and thwarted attempts at revenge, drinking away a fair amount of his brother's earnings. He had inquired of everyone he met as to the whereabouts of Alouicious Rucker, but the men of the area seemed to have no concern for anything but silver, and no one would admit to having heard of the man. So Logan sank deeper into a funk, having no trail to follow and fearing to head for any more populous area as the law would surely be looking for him. His defeat settled onto his shoulders like a great weight and he spent most of his days sitting on an empty keg behind his brother's tent swilling the dreadful forty rod the teamsters brought in, which was where he was when he happened to glance up and through a haze of whiskey see none other than Alouicious Rucker and the reporter he had shot in Santa Fe dismounting in front of a nearby shack which served as the local saloon.

Abel was having a good day at the card table as several teamsters had arrived earlier and unloaded their overpriced trade goods on the miners before stopping for a quick game of poker before heading back for another load. Le'Chiffre sat at the other table, doing and equally brisk trade and the two were so engrossed in the game that both gamblers were startled when Logan bellowed from his usual perch behind the tent.

"Rucker!" the sot shouted simply, making Abel think that his brother had finally gone completely mad, but the shouting continued:

"Get ready to meet your maker, you son of a

bitch!"

"I fold" said Abel simply, mucking his cards and rising calmly to his feet.

"Are you sure you want to go out there, Abel?" asked Le'Chiffre, still sitting at the other table.

"I have to, he's my brother,"

"Damn," said Jean-Batiste rising from his seat "I'll be back presently" he said to the teamsters who were staring curiously at the pair before taking up his shotgun and checking the load.

"You don't have to come with me," said Abel drawing his pistol.

"Just shut up and let's go" said an irritated Le'Chiffre.

As the two men rounded the tent they saw the tableau they had feared as Rucker and Logan had squared off in the muddy area between tents which passed for a street in the camp. Neither man had yet to draw a weapon, but both were at the ready, standing as statues as if waiting for a cue.

"You boys stay out of this," called Logan seeing his brother and Le'Chiffre out of the corner of his eye.

"Yes, do stay where you are," said Peabody from across the street as he leveled his shotgun at the pair. Abel and Jean-Batiste halted at the sight of the reporter and made no move as they glanced back and forth between Ruck and Logan who still had eyes only for one another.

"We don't have to do this," said Ruck, not understanding the depth of Logan's hatred.

"Oh but we do," replied Logan with a drunken grin "and after I'm finished with you I'm gonna hunt down that filthy Indian Kessay and scalp him and his whole family, only then will this be finished."

Logan never knew the fatal mistake he was making as he uttered the threat, since Ruck's expression did not waver; he gave no cry, voiced no denial, indeed he gave no warning whatsoever before calmly and smoothly drawing his pistol and shooting Logan in the chest.

Ruck's movement was so sudden and fluid that the spectators were stunned, all three standing with mouths agape as Ruck calmly re-cocked the hammer on his pistol, maintaining his bead on Logan as the outlaw fell. Logan had reached his pistol but had only drawn it part way from the holster before Ruck's bullet struck him like lightning, robbing him of first the strength to retaliate and then his life.

As it became clear that Logan would not be getting up again, Ruck smoothly swung his pistol to his right, bringing it to bear on Abel and Jean-Batiste who were still standing aghast.

"Are you boys next?" Ruck asked in tones which betrayed no fear.

Abel was still speechless, but Jean-Batiste recovered from the shock enough to drop his shotgun to the ground and take his friend's arm.

"Gentlemen, I believe our business is concluded. Come along Abel, I believe we're wanted inside," he said tipping his hat to Ruck and Peabody before leading Abel away from the grisly sight of his brother lying dead in the street.

As the two men disappeared around the corner of the tent, Peabody rushed toward Ruck, arriving just as he lowered his pistol. Ruck's hands were shaking visibly and he had trouble holstering his gun as tears began streaming down his face.

"That was the most amazing thing I have ever seen" exclaimed Peabody before he saw the stricken look on Ruck's face.

"I don't feel well" said Ruck simply before bending at the waist and being violently sick in the street.

"I imagine you don't," said Peabody patting him on the back compassionately "come, let's go get a drink, shall we?"

Seeing that the commotion had died down, the denizens of the camp began to emerge from concealment all around them. Crowding around, the men patted Ruck on the back and took turns shaking his hand, congratulating him on his fine marksmanship and promising to testify that the shooting had been in self defense if the matter ever came to the attention of the authorities. Peabody did his best to ward off the well wishers, trying to give the still distraught Ruck room to breathe, but the ebullient mob could not be dissuaded from following the two men into the saloon offering to buy Ruck many rounds of whiskey to celebrate his victory. Ruck felt neither celebratory nor victorious but he accepted a drink or two at Peabody's insistence which did little to quiet his troubled nerves.

All eyes were on the hero of the hour, so only Bolliver was watching as Whitey inspected the corpse lying in the street. The dog sniffed Logan's body for some time, until apparently satisfied that they would receive no more trouble from the outlaw, Whitey lifted his leg and peed on the dead man. Bolliver and Sunshine looked at each other and nickered in the manner of horse laughter.

Dawn the next day found Peabody and Ruck once again on the road, this time headed east. The men had spent a tense night in Globe, not knowing if Abel would try to extract some vengeance for his brother's death, but morning had arrived with no sign of vendetta and the two men saddled their horses in unspoken agreement to leave the town of Globe for good.

Ruck had calmed considerably since the dire events of the day before, but was still discomforted by the thought that he had taken a man's life. He knew that if he had not shot Logan, the outlaw would probably have done so to him, and possibly even worse to Kessay and Magashi, but Ruck was no killer, and he lamented having to do such a thing. Despite his melancholy over the shooting, Ruck felt happy at the thought that he would soon see Magashi again, and he desperately hoped she would forgive him for his mistake of leaving in the first place.

Peabody had no such reservations about the death of such a terrible villain as Logan Beckwith, and was overjoyed to be headed back toward his beloved Eunice once again. His earlier disillusionment with the man he had built up as an idol was replaced with the respect of a man he had come to call his friend, and Peabody renewed his commitment to write a book about Ruck now that he knew the real story.

As the two rode into the rising sun, they exchanged anecdotes about their respective loves, and both promised to visit the other if the chance arose, knowing that such a thing was unlikely. Not long into the ride the two men reached the rim of a mighty canyon, whose walls plunged hundreds of feet to the Salt River below.

"Looks like this is where we part company," said Ruck taking in the majestic vista of the canyon.

"I guess it is," replied Peabody wistfully, wishing there was more to say.

"Well, so long Peabody, it's been a pleasure" said Ruck as he turned Bolliver to follow the canyon to the south.

"Adios Ruck," called Peabody turning Sunshine to the north.

As the two men parted company, Peabody could hear the sound of Ruck whistling as he rode away. He smiled when he identified the tune and he likewise began to whistle the opening strains of 'The Girl I Left Behind Me.'

The End